"If you love Grindhouse movies and miss monsters and mayhem at the drive-in, this is the perfect summer book; a nostalgic back-to-the-80s trip to a Florida beach stocked with beasts and breasts and soaked with blood and booze. "

Steve Latshaw
Author, Stan Lee's LIGHTSPEED

# DEEP RED

— . —

## Based on a story by Edward D Wood, Jr

## Fred Olen Ray

RETROMEDIA PRESS

www.retromediapress.com

sales@retromedia.org

Print ISBN: 979-8-9865215-2-7

eBook ISBN: 979-8-9865215-3-4

First Edition

For Martin Nicholas, Richard Gabai and Steve Latshaw
They know where the bodies are buried

# FOREWORD

In late summer of 1978, two filmmakers put their creative heads together to devise a new creature feature.

One, an old pro who had been out of the spotlight for decades. The other, an aspiring 23-year-old kid with dreams of a career in motion pictures.

The old pro was Edward D. Wood, Jr. The kid was me.

My plan was to align myself with someone who possessed recognizable film credits. I thought it might help me, a young inexperienced nobody, raise the financing I desired for a low-budget horror film.

Ed Wood was not the Ed Wood fans would later come to idolize. He was not yet the subject of books, magazine articles or film retrospectives. I've often thought about how giddy Eddie would have been had he just lived long enough to see everything go down. Sadly, while fame was just around the corner, it was, for Ed, a corner too far. There was even a major biopic about his life produced by Tim Burton. They titled it ED WOOD (1994).

In 1978 Ed was a 54-year-old, past-his-prime writer-producer-director, living check to check from his rapid-fire work on questionable projects of a pornographic nature.

To me, Ed Wood was the mastermind behind the Bela
Lugosi thrillers, BRIDE OF THE MONSTER (1955) and PLAN
NINE FROM OUTER SPACE (1957). Neither was considered
a classic, but in my eyes, they might be just the springboard
I needed.

In all honesty, I hadn't seen either film in ages, but that
wasn't the point. I didn't care what their shortcomings
might have been. Little did I know.

*Bela Lugosi looks on as his agent signs with Ed Wood Jr.*

A mutual friend introduced me to Wood, and we hit it
off. I agreed to pay Eddie five hundred dollars to write a
screenplay we called BEACH BLANKET BLOODBATH.

If successful, I intended to shoot the movie in Florida.
It concerned a lab-created Shark Man. A hideous, walk-

ing beast dressed in medical scrubs, ala THE CREATURE WALKS AMONG US (1956), featuring a shark's dorsal fin jutting from its spine.

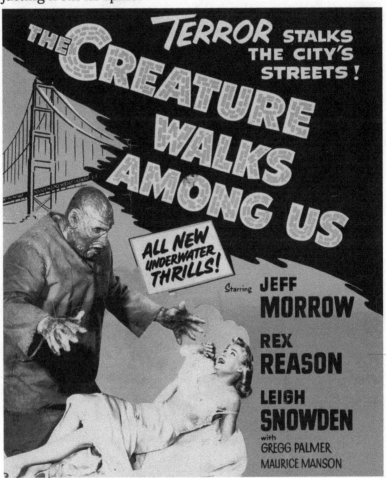

As the holidays approached, I mailed Eddie a Christmas card and waited for the script to roll in. Work would be slightly delayed, he explained, by the need to have his typewriter repaired. Later, I was informed; he had actually pawned the machine, his primary source of income, for booze money.

Leading up to December, we conducted several script confabs, arriving at what we believed to be a good story.

Once settled on the plot, I started sculpting a full-head mask for the shark man at my kitchen table. Back in the early days, I did my own makeup effects work.

A few weeks into December, Ed's Christmas card was returned to me. "Moved. No Forwarding Address." I panicked. I phoned our friend, who said, "Yeah, Eddie died." And that was that.

Six years later, I took the original story we had cobbled together and wrote my own screenplay based on it. I called it BLOOD TIDE. I never made the movie, but I used the story and screenplay as the outline for my novel, DEEP RED. Published here for the first time.

I wove in the H. P. Lovecraft influences during the novelization phase because his short story, THE SHADOW OVER INNSMOUTH, was my favorite and seemed suited for the story.

The two wicked, lesbian mad doctors are pure Ed Wood.

I have never made this novel available in any format prior to this publishing and do so now as a curiosity piece. I make no representations as to its literary quality or entertainment value.

As a matter of record, I would like to clarify that Ed Wood wrote not a single word of this novel, but as it is based on a story Eddie and I wiggled out years ago, I believed he deserved acknowledgment.

# CHAPTER ONE

— • —

The Journal of Dr. John Richard Ashley

July 1935

S OMEONE SNAPPED ON A bright light and I shut my eyes, holding up my hand as if to fight off the searing brightness.

"Give it a moment," a voice said. "You'll adjust to it."

And I did.

When I dared to crack my eyelids, I discovered that the light wasn't as blinding, or as brilliant, as I had first perceived it to be. It was, in fact, nothing more than a small battery of common photo-flood lamps, the kind often associated with still photographers. They were brutal because of the darkness they had kept me in for the last hour and a half.

My eyes adjusted, but I could see where they had brought me. It was a barren space, small with a curious, noxious smell.

The floor was unfinished wood planks and the walls, wooden as well, were a drab military green. The entire space smelled of tar, not unlike the lower quarters of an old sailing ship.

Frankly, I was at a complete loss where I was. For now, that was their secret.

Everything was a secret, everything except who they were. They would be hard to keep out. In fact, I'm not overstating things when I tell you the state leader who stood a few feet from me was one of the most powerful men in the world, and while I am sworn not to repeat names, I believe the details, little as I know of them, should be committed to paper. Maybe one day some poor fool will read this and care.

On an overcast afternoon, in a week of gloomy days, I received a letter, hand delivered by a stony-faced young man in a natty suit. He insisted I read it while he waited. Beyond him at the curb, I spied an elegant roadster of remarkable design and the dark shapes of at least two other gentlemen. I tried not to stare, but the young man caught me and smiled. I smiled back and invited him to step inside.

With the door closed, I moved to my favorite chair and offered him a seat on the couch.

"I'll stand, sir," he said. I gathered he was more than eager for me to get on with it, so I unsealed the envelope and removed its contents. The young man wandered over to my aquarium. A large one, I'm proud to say, and populated by some very rare specimens. He leaned close to the glass face and stared into the water. He muttered something in a low voice after tapping on the glass.

I didn't know what to make of the letter. It was a summons of sorts, a stern one, to accompany this young man, whom the letter identified as a Special Government Agent, to an undisclosed location where I would meet a past acquaintance of mine, Dr. Rodman Weatherall. That's all it said..

Oh yes, it also said I was required to accept this invitation.

I slid the letter back into its envelope and looked at the junior agent, who smiled again and flashed me an important-looking badge, which I was certain he polished daily. I assumed I had already accepted the invitation.

"You'll need your coat and hat, Professor," he said matter-of-factly. "I'll get them for you."

Once in the car, a silken sleeping mask was placed over my eyes. I uttered a slight protest but was assured it was for my good.

The two men were not speaking.

After placing the soft mask over my eyes, I felt the car jolt as it pulled away from the curb.

I was seeing the entire room now. It was dim under the stark, eerie glow of the bare photofloods. Several shapes stood ringed about me. A few were in starched white lab coats, some in high-ranking military finery, ribbons, medals, and such. And, of course, there was the state leader I referred to earlier.

At the center of the room was a large, uncovered glass tank in the shape of a coffin, but with low sides, perhaps thirty inches high. They had filled the tank to the brim with an unidentified fluid. It might have been water, alcohol, or some other clear liquid. I remember it gave off a peculiar stringent odor that I was unfamiliar with. It resembled a chemical bath, and the smell curled my nostrils. What I saw laying submerged in the liquid tank was nightmarish.

Dr. Rodman Weatherall stepped forward from the small gaggle of white coats and approached me, a welcoming hand out-stretched.

"Richard... God, how long has it been?" he asked, his voice sounding exhausted.

I smiled. "At least four years, Rodman. But..."

He held up a halting hand. "I know you're full of questions, and you deserve answers, but save them for later, I beg you."

I nodded and studied the other alert faces surrounding me. They impressed me.

"You'll excuse me if I don't introduce everyone," he continued. "No names here... I'm sure you understand."

Of course I didn't understand, but names weren't necessary. I recognized most of these people, anyway.

They were all very newsworthy.

"We can catch up on old times later," he said, smiling. "I want to show you something and you can tell me your thoughts."

Everybody was smiling, like it was the happiest place on Earth. I might have found some humor in my concern about my well-being. The false, strained politeness, the mandatory handshakes and fake smiles. The men looked more nervous than I did.

I squinted under the harsh lights, looking to where Rodman pointed... the large glass tank. Something was poking out, bobbing, just above the surface of the fluid. It looked like the top of a submerged tree stump. Ashen gray and knobby.

"This entire business has my head spinning, Rodman. Am I to be made a prisoner?"

"Of course not, Richard. Please... just have a look."

And look I did.

Within the liquid floated something preserved. A shape. Humanoid but altered in ways that would be hard to describe. The body was like a dead shark left in the sun. Wrinkled and leathery. I thought that what was in that tank was dead.

Its head was narrow, with large protruding eyes that were positioned at least six inches apart. Its pupils were clouded with a thick milky coating, but from what I could determine, they were human.

The ears were tiny, almost not ears at all, and beneath them were gaping rows of split skin folds resembling the gills of an eel. The twisted anatomy of the specimen was perplexing me, but I figured it was some kind of mutation, or perhaps a species not yet documented by science, at least not the science they invested me in.

The most important man asked if I'd heard of Innsmouth. "Innsmouth, Massachusetts?"

Before answering, all eyes were on me.

"No, I don't think so. Should I have?"

No one spoke for a long moment. They looked like they were reading each other's mind. Then my old friend Weatherall jumped in to pick up the slack.

"Back in February of '28 a little dust-up erupted along the coast of New England. Just beyond the village of Innsmouth. A rotten place. The services of some of the country's finest fighting men were required. You see, it was all very secretive. It is classified, but not without its interesting side."

Rodman looked at the preserved specimen floating in the tank. The odor of chemicals seemed to delight, rather than repel him.

"What they found there in Innsmouth and its neighboring marshes would curl your hair. It did mine," he said.

"The town was a crumbling wreck of discarded businesses and disheveled dwellings that might have stood for God knows how long if not for an alarm being raised by a terrified traveler who'd become stranded. Poor fellow escaped with his life... or so he said. An FBI investigation uncovered something extraordinary lurking under the surface. Bizarre stuff. I'm not at liberty to discuss the affair, Richard... it's on a need-to-know basis, you understand... but I can tell you this... the thing in front of you lived in one of the finer homes in town."

"That?" I asked, pointing at the hideous shape submerged in the tank.

"And it wasn't alone," the supreme state leader broke in. "There were... hundreds of them in various stages of development."

"Some pregnant," one officer of ridiculously high rank added.

"Dynamite," Weatherall snapped. "They dynamited the whole place. Took it off the map."

"Had to blow the reef with depth charges," a voice at the back added.

"Correct," agreed Rodman. "There was a submerged reef off the coast of Innsmouth. Devil's Reef, they called it. Goddamned place was crawling with these things. Killed them all... or at least we hope so."

I stared again at the hideous body floating in the tank. I shuddered to think these creatures were breeding in that sleepy New England town. Well away from prying eyes.

"What a horrible thought," I heard myself mumble.

"Horrible is right," reckoned Weatherall. "But not without interest, eh?"

"And the survivors? What became of them?" I asked.

"A handful of... 'citizens' were moved to a concentration camp down South for study. It was an unfortunate decision... unfortunate. The occupants of the town where we "relocated" the subjects became very disturbed. Claimed the Innsmouth folks were practicing a sorcery... cult worship. Many believed the town's women were being mesmerized into having immoral "relations" with a few of the human-looking types and, well..."

"A riot broke out," a General interjected. "In one night, the entire containment camp was burned to the ground by vigilantes... Every prisoner from Innsmouth was destroyed. It was a night of horrifying events, most of them best not described, but you can hardly blame them. The whole affair was a bad idea from the start."

I drew in a deep breath. "What do you want from me, Rodman?" I asked.

"This is our last viable specimen. They dissected the others for research and, in doing so, we learned a very serious lesson."

"And that is?"

"The aquatic mutating traits of this... sub-race... can be transmitted like a virus into an open wound."

"You're joking?"

"You can be exposed to the strain if you have one minor cut on your finger. We lost quite a few talented doctors, thanks to these devils."

"All dead?"

"We're not sure, but we're certain of one thing... if there is a use for this mutating gene, we need to find it, isolate it and control it."

"A use?" Did I hear him correctly?

"In the interest of National security, of course," said the state leader.

"Of course," I said. "But what's this to do with me?"

"We're more than aware of your expertise in marine biology, Richard," Weatherall smiled. "Together, you and I can preserve a sampling of tissue matter and blood from this subject. We'll isolate the active agent, if possible."

I nodded, realizing after hearing this, there was no way out for me. I had to comply, and I did. If God, in his infinite *wisdom, had looked down upon us that day, he would have been grinning, for everything we attempted in the weeks to come met with miserable failure.*

*The work was gruesome. Unlike anything I'd ever been involved in before. And the fetuses. Innsmouth fetuses, snatched from the wombs of some god-awful she-things, staring with sightless, unblinking eyes from their formalin specimen jars. Large, fishy eyes watched me as I whittled away at the corpse on the table in front of me.*

*Dissection was slow and unpleasant. The constant presence of thick protective gloves and body suits made the work torturous within the stifling climate of the odorous tar-soaked wooden bunker.*

*In the third week, my mind became unhinged. It was more of a nagging feeling in the second week. In the third week, I performed a procedure on the specimen that verified all of my inner horror. In that third week, as I placed my scalpel against the leathery skin and began making my incision to remove the heart, I discovered to my horror that the withered body of the piteous thing from Innsmouth, the thing I had been dissecting into tiny fragments for almost three long weeks, was still alive!*

*Thankfully, on the very next day, as evening was just setting in, the entire facility caught fire under questionable circumstances and the cleansing flames swept through the building like a fiery rake, taking with it the final judgment on the Innsmouth blood.*

*Professor John Richard Ashley*

A ND THERE THE WRITTEN account concluded. The loose sheets of paper slid back into the envelope.

"Where did you find this?" Daniels asked.

"It came through messenger, sir," replied a young non-com. "I believe it was beneath a drawer in the old records building. Apparently, the hanging files in the rack above it had obscured the envelope. What should we do with it?"

Major Daniels stroked his chin. The incident at Innsmouth was never an acceptable subject of discussion.

"Hell, it's been over a half century since all that happened," he mused. "It implicates some people pretty high up. I wonder who they were?"

The young non-com shifted, awaiting an order.

"Better leave it with me, son," Daniels said. "And don't mention it to anyone. You never found it. Understood?"

The officer saluted. "Yes, sir."

"That is all."

When the young officer left, Daniels picked up the envelope. It was old and yellowed. He wondered how it had fallen into the hands of the authorities, and for one moment, he pondered the fate of Professor John Richard Ashley. Daniels knew there was nothing to gain from reviving the Innsmouth incident. It was dangerous to think about.

He took the envelope down into the lower depths of the building; into that area of locked files that no one ever dared open. He found the proper cabinet and used a special key only a few men in the government knew about. Within that drawer were the documents pertaining to the cataclysmic military assault on Innsmouth, Massachusetts, in the winter of 1928. Here, at the back of the drawer, far from curious eyes, he deposited the envelope.

Daniels hoped that perhaps another fifty years would pass before anyone delved into these records again. Let them remain here. Hidden. Safe from anyone ever discovering the lurid details of what had transpired during that dark time in the past, when sea-creatures passed as human, and humans passed as beasts.

# CHAPTER TWO

—·—

D R. SYLVIA TRENT'S FINGER was tight on the trigger. She looked down the lonely corridor. She saw nothing. No sign of life, but it didn't fool her. She knew better.

If it wasn't here, then it was somewhere close by. And it was clever.

She didn't want to kill, but she was prepared, even anxious, to put a blast of buckshot into anything that stirred in the gloom beyond her.

Her fingers gripped the polished wood stock. The muscles in her young arms taut and ready to spring. Perspiration trickled between her panting breasts, leaving an icy trail that crept all the way to her navel.

She hadn't had time to dress when the alarm first sounded and now she crouched low behind the door frame in sweat-dampened panties, hefting a twelve-gauge shotgun with five shells in its gut and one in the chamber. She wasn't one for taking chances. Danger excited her. The adrenaline rush of fear was foreplay to her. She tingled as she shifted the gun from her shoulder to a cradle at her hip, her nipples tight with the unrestrained chill of terror.

Sylvia must have been dreaming when the trouble started... a sex dream that hadn't quite washed away. She noticed wetness beneath her arms and on her forehead. It felt like a climax of pleasure and pain. That thing was in here somewhere, waiting to kill, and the thought of dying stirred a cascade of emotions.

All she hoped for was survival. That the horror would disappear on its own. She wondered where Gail was. The girl was always within arm's length of Sylvia whenever she awoke, but now there was no sign of her.

Maybe Gail was dead.

Sylvia backed up a few steps, satisfied that the danger was not within immediate striking distance. She doubled back to safety, hoping to find Gail, if she could.

The building was a maze-like structure of twisted corridors, untenanted rooms and laboratory spaces. Where once many people had worked in scientific research, now there were two. Security amounted to little more than a sophisticated lock outside and a loaded shotgun inside.

All the trouble was inside.

Sylvia returned to the primary control and found no sign of Gail. She punched up the closed-circuit monitoring system, but all that emitted from the screens was a static hissing and video snow. From those in working condition, she could hear sounds from the other checkpoints.

They revealed nothing from those sectors except a small scraping sound in the back loading bay, the one that gave exit to the seaward side of the facility.

"I hope that's not what I think it is," Sylvia muttered under her breath.

Sylvia took off towards the loading bay, shotgun thrust forward, ready to cut anything she encountered in half. She only hoped that Gail wouldn't come running out unexpectedly.

Sylvia was very fond of Gail.

When she caught sight of the loading bay door, she realized the nightmare had ended, at least for the moment, anyway. The morning sun poured through the door, blinding her. The jagged hole torn in the metal by some dominant force was large and accommodating. Blood dripped from the sharper jagged edges of the twisted metal. Anything could have fit through it.

The sea breeze rifled down the corridor like an over-worked air conditioner, sending yet another chill through Sylvia's glistening body. The perspiration dried and goosebumps sprang up on her naked skin.

Whatever had roamed the halls of the Triton Project was gone now, and Sylvia felt an exasperated sigh slip through her lips. She shivered.

Then she heard the sound.

Low at first, then louder and with growing intensity. An urgent scraping, scratching sound. Sylvia looked around, listening. It appeared to come from the maintenance door.

She pressed her ear to the door, reassuring herself this was, in fact, the source of the disturbance. She hesitated when the door opened from the hall, fearing what might happen on the other side. Sylvia aimed the shotgun at the door after the scraper stopped. Her finger squeezed the trigger.

"Sylvia!" came an anguished cry from within.

"Jesus Christ! Gail!"

Sylvia yanked the door open, letting young Gail Anders tumble forward onto her hands and knees. Like Sylvia, she was all but naked as she crouched animal-like and sucked in huge gulps of air, her body shaking with fear.

Sylvia knelt down beside her, placing a supporting arm around her shoulders.

"Are you all right?"

"I am now," Gail gasped, her eyes streaked with tears, her lips moist and full.

Sylvia helped the girl to her feet.

"What the hell happened?" she asked, pressing Gail's trembling body against her own.

"It broke into my room! All I could do was escape. I ran to the loading bay. I thought I might get outside, but the doors took too long to unlock, so I hid in the maintenance room."

"Which is soundproof."

"Right, but it only reopens from the inside with a key. I thought if it couldn't hear me, I might have a chance. After I heard it rip through the bay doors, I knew it was gone and all I could do was scrape at the door, hoping you'd hear me."

Sylvia held Gail close and pressed the young girl's head to her shoulder. "It's all right now. We're safe."

"What are we going to do?" Gail asked, pressing even tighter into Sylvia's warm flesh.

Sylvia held her away and looked into Gail's eyes. "First," she said. "We're going to repair the bay doors... somehow, and we will not breathe a word of this to anyone. You understand?"

"We're the only ones who know what is happening," Gail said.

"It needs to stay that way."

Gail looked frightened as a new, terrifying thought raced through her mind. Sylvia saw that look and meant to squelch it.

"Don't start, Gail! You know we can't tell anyone and besides, it can't live out there on its own. It will die within six hours... trust me. So stop worrying, okay?"

Gail nodded but didn't agree. She knew full well what had escaped through that armor-plated door. She knew what the horror could do to a person.

What if the thing didn't die? She wondered. What if it survived? What would happen when it grew hungry? Gail couldn't bring herself to even think about it. They were alive, and that's what mattered at the moment. She could pray everything would work out as Sylvia had said, but then, trembling in the hallway, she wasn't sure.

"Come on. Get dressed," Sylvia said. "We've got cleaning to do."

# Chapter Three

— • —

M IKE REARDON COULD SEE it in the center of the road fifty yards ahead. A small, garden variety tortoise.

With slow determination, the tortoise had made its way to the center of the road. It was sunny and warm, perfect for soaking up the heat from the tarmac. Tortoises crossed this road often, without incident... until Mike Reardon came along.

The rising warmth felt good against its little leather-padded feet and when it arrived at the double yellow line, it crept to a halt and rested for a while.

Mike grinned, jamming the accelerator of his battle-scarred Corvair hard to the floor. Mike wanted the speed today. Today, he wanted to scream. Today, he held an anger inside him that no amount of hard driving could wrench from his gut. Being caught in a no-win situation gave him that anger and helplessness. For a young man in control of his life, and occasionally the lives of a few others, he now found himself in the grip of strangers. It was a sour, hateful feeling, and he didn't tolerate it well.

Mike was a young man with a taste for women. Folks reckoned it was his personality. His "talent", as he liked to refer to it, more often than not, caused considerable complication in his life. He had a hank of sandy blond hair, well chiseled features and a sporting build. He was also a little cocky, and he knew that too.

On this day, summer of '83, he was on the road to Pine Level, Florida. It was his first assignment since graduating from the Florida State Police Academy and he hated it, which was fine because he was supposed to hate it. It was a punishment. A loud, painful, and very public smack in the face, and he despised everything associated with it. He kept thinking about it as he pressed the gas pedal hard, holding it steady at top speed.

Mike bore down on the unsuspecting terrapin like a rocket, twisting the wheel at the last possible moment, whizzing past the tortoise. Maybe next time, Mike thought as he shot by the weathered sign that showed the approach to Pine Level.

Like the tortoise, life at Pine Level had crawled to a standstill. Mike had heard rumors about it at the Police Sciences Academy. It was a favorite dumping site for difficult recruits with a black mark on their permanent record. A few months in this coastal backwater ghost town was enough to knock the stuffing out of any snotty kid's sails.

Mike glanced in his rear view mirror at the indiscriminate idiot who had gotten him into this mess. Cute guy, he thought, uppity with a side order of stupid to go... all the qualifications required to get your ass dunked for six months in Pine Level instead of one of those desirable big city assignments. He ran his fingers through his windblown hair. Ft. Lauderdale would seem like heaven right about now.

Turning off the main drag onto the rough road towards town, he couldn't help but notice the wide range of deserted shacks and vacant businesses that littered the landscape, their broken windowpanes staring out at passers-by with empty eye sockets. The freeway had long since passed these bad boys by in the wake of progress and Pine Level, for all its ancient promises, had withdrawn into its husk like a salted snail.

Mike received a file on the village and, thin as it was, it showed the place to be no different from dozens of other clumps of withered civilization that peppered the gulf coast north of Tampa. The advance dossier mentioned the pothole's brief history as the rebel stronghold of pirate Captain Jose Gaspar in the late 1880s. Since those rousing times, when blood and sex intermingled like heady mead, Pine Level had stopped partying. Very little in the way of raping and pillaging had been going on there of late. In fact, the only people who visited the community now were a handful of lost vacationers and a few sport fishers who wandered in when the Kingfish and Bonitos were plentiful; this was not nearly that time of the year.

After twenty minutes of dodging the weed-sprouting cracks in the crumbling asphalt, Mike saw a small roadside gas station approaching fast. A wooden sign, held together by its very splinters, promised that *Live Wrigglers & Shiners* could be had for a modest stipend inside. Mike grinned at the simplicity of the sign and its painted message and turned the radio down.

As he pulled into the crushed shell parking lot, he realized the joint was empty. Not a car in sight. He looked around for a spark of life.

Nothing.

The gas pumps were antiques, but functional, so he grabbed the Regular nozzle and pushed it deep into the Corvair. Nothing beat a classic car that still enjoyed the taste of a regular octane cocktail. It was the greatest car Mike had ever owned. The scent of a dozen rookie police-women lingered on the tuck-and-roll upholstery. The car was his baby, his woman, and his mother, all wrapped up in one wheezing tumor on wheels. Rust was the only thing holding her together.

Mike kept glancing around the deserted station as he pumped the gas. It was better than free sex. The hose jerked spastically in his hand as it struggled to spurt the fuel into the thirsty tank.

He figured someone was bound to show up to collect the money, but no one appeared and it tempted him to jump back in the car and take off. He fought back the larcenous urge and made a quick search for the attendant. After all, he was the new police photographer; it wouldn't do for him to be pinched on a misdemeanor before he even got to town.

He climbed the grey, warped steps into a small shack that appeared to be the station office, but there was nothing inside except a rack of dusty oil cans coated with a thick layer of grime, a faded calendar featuring a topless chick with breasts larger than her head in a mechanics' coverall, and an old web lawn chair with a case of the rots. Left of the parking lot, he saw another outbuilding, the *Bait Bucket*, a dingy wooden hovel that looked like a slaughterhouse for marine by-products.

As he walked towards it, he heard a sharp noise rankle out. Something had fallen inside with a loud clatter. It sounded like a couple of metal garbage cans being tossed into the back of a pickup truck.

"Hello," Mike called, but got no response. "Hey, I pumped some gas out here. Don't you want your money?"

No one answered. Instead, he heard a new sound jolt out of the shack. Something thrashed about inside, followed by the bending snapping of old dry wood. Mike didn't want to look inside. He shivered when he thought about what might happen in there. His mind raced back to the Police Academy casebooks and the stories about crazed cannibalistic hillbillies who murdered passing tourists and made book covers and sausages out their remains... and that was before being sexually assaulted by them and their kinfolk.

Not today, thank you.

Mike's nervous curiosity got the better of him, but curious or not, he still waited a full thirty seconds after the last shrieking, rending sound had been unleashed before making any move to enter.

He placed a foot on the rickety porch, resulting in a low, ominous, alarming creak. He didn't even breathe, he just waited and listened. Nothing stirred inside. Whatever it was, had heard his footsteps. Maybe it was behind the door. Maybe ten seconds from now he would be headcheese.

Then he detected a low, weird gurgling sound moan within the darkness. Poking his head in, he saw the aftermath of the violence. Tin bait cans were crushed on the floor and newspapers scattered. Since something had shattered the lamp in the disturbance, the light was dim. Mike could see puddles of water covering the floor. The low bubbling, moaning sound was coming from an antique pump that chugged air into the series of open steel troughs that kept the bait alive.

Most of the bait fish and shrimp were not in their troughs, however. They were flopping on the floor of the tar-paper shack, wheezing out their last breath. Those not fighting for their lives were already dead, their heads torn off and discarded about the room. Minnow blood mingled with salt-water on the floor, creating a very distinctive, suffocating odor like Thursday afternoon at a cut-rate sushi joint.

Mike felt sick. He took a quick look around and noted a large hole in the back wall where the boards had been ripped away, creating a huge gaping wound. He didn't know what had come in or gone out, but his curiosity ended where the jagged boards began.

"Goddamnedest mess I ever see'd," came a scruffy voice behind him. If a voice could be described as scruffy, this was it. Mike nearly jumped out of his skin.

"Didn't mean to scare you, son."

Mike stared over his shoulder at the backlit shape etched in the doorway. It was a man. Spindly and unstable, but human. The shape stepped where Mike could see him a bit more clearly. Besides everything else, he looked to be at least 80 years old. For a moment, Mike stared at the old man.

"I didn't do this," Mike fumbled. "I came looking for someone to give the gas money after I heard something moving."

The old man looked at the damage.

"I don't know what done this," he said, shaking his head. "But I believe it wasn't you."

Mike relaxed a little. "Yeah," he responded. "Looks like somebody went fishing... indoors."

"I reckon it's like you say, kid," the old man replied, rubbing the unshaven bristle on his chin.

"Maybe a bear or a panther," Mike suggested. "Probably smelled the bait a mile away."

"Maybe, but I think we'd all be surprised at what kind of critter come through that wall today."

"Well, that hole suggests something large waltzed in here for a little whirlwind shopping and took the fire exit," Mike offered, pointing at the torn opening in the back wall.

"You must be some kind of city fella," the man said, puzzled by Mike's choice of words. "Tourist?"

Mike flipped out his shiny, newly gained badge and flashed it at the old man.

"Cop, huh?"

"Sort of, yeah."

"Good. Then you come around here to the backside," the old man said, motioning Mike to follow. "I want to show you something real unnatural."

The old guy climbed off the porch and crept back behind the bait shack. Mike was afraid of what he might have put his foot in. The going was tough through the overgrown weeds and discarded tractor parts, but the jungle of rubbish subsided in the high grass at the back of the building.

The thick growth had been beaten down to a crop circle below the rip in the shack. He looked at the sharp wood fragments that jutted from the rickety frame like jagged knife blades. The edges were wet and covered with some kind of wet pulpy tissue. Mike sidled up to the opening for a closer view. The more wicked-looking spines had snagged the black, tar-like tissue. It dripped an amber syrupy fluid down the side of the shack and reeked of spoilt meat. Black and slimy like an eel. He reached out to pluck off a piece, but his hand wavered.

"God, I don't think I can touch that," he said, shaking his head. "I'm not a lab tech, you know."

"No need to touch it," the old man explained. "I can tell you what it feels like."

"How's that?"

"I felt it yesterday," the man replied. "Felt just like a grinding disk. Rough and scratchy-like..."

"No shit? Maybe it's just some tar-paper insulation from inside the wall. Tar-paper with mold growing on it."

The old man didn't seem to accept Mike's prognosis. "Look here," he continued, pointing to the weeds beneath the hole. "Something big has been through here... twice, at least. Hell, that hole got ripped open just yesterday morning! It was only making it *bigger* today."

Mike looked where the man pointed and saw some large indentations in the muck and weeds. They looked like footprints. Fifteen inches long, five feet between strides, he guessed.

"See," Mike said, standing up. "I told you it was a bear. These prints prove it."

"It weren't nary no bear," the old man argued. "And that ain't no tar-paper hanging off'n them splinters."

"Look, if something had busted in here yesterday, why not just wait until it came back and catch it in the act?"

"Too busy hiding under the shed... you're a cop. Why don't you do something about it?"

"I only shoot things with a camera, but I'm sure once I get into town I'll find somebody who can take care of this problem. You got a phone?"

"Out by the road, but come here first," the old man insisted.

Mike walked behind the man as he tread a path through the high weeds into the woods beyond. After about twenty yards of tangled foliage, the trail opened up on a small inlet. The crushing prints led down to the sand and into the water. They didn't come back out.

"That bear must have had some scuba-gear, you reckon?" the old man cackled.

Mike looked over at the scene. "You know, I probably had enough gas to get me into town. I didn't even need to stop here, so please buddy, just take your money," he insisted, shoving the old man a ten spot, "and get yourself a good, steel-jawed leg-hold trap. Bury it in back of your place and quit hiding under the shed, okay? It's not healthy."

Mike stomped through the weeds, back to his car, and drove off. This was his M.O., he thought. The same stupid, nonsensical poking-around-where-he-didn't-belong that had gotten him into trouble so many times before. Why couldn't he just leave well enough alone? Why did he have to look in the bait shop? He could have just minded his own business and kept going. If he'd done that a month earlier when a sweet little something had whispered in his ear, he wouldn't be driving along this deserted, bone-dry road in the middle of nowhere right now.

Yeah, this is stupid, he thought, but he had to admit it was a damned strange bit of stupid he'd just walked away from. One that might require some looking into later, but now it was nearing dusk on a late Sunday afternoon and his focus was on locating a cheap motel, a shower to wash away the odor of dead fish and bite to eat. He had to report to his new boss in the morning, and while he had few hopes for this town or his assignment, he didn't want to be late on his first day. He knew that word had preceded him and there was no need to make a poor situation worse.

As he drove through the descending gloom, he passed a large disused area surrounded by a high barb-wire enclosure. A group of shacks surrounded by a rusty fence appeared to be primitive. The whole place, a large compound at one time, had been deserted for years, overgrown with weeds. The small, warped buildings rotted and sagging under their own weight.

Mike looked away from what must have been, in the old days, a migrant fruit picker's camp and flipped the radio on. It played nothing but white noise.

Up ahead, as the sun waned, the glare of the Corvair's headlights revealed another turtle in the road. This one wasn't moving either. It was dead.

# Chapter Four

— · —

I N THE BLACKNESS, A hissing neon flashed. The colors were putrescent, but they were very real. In between the flickering and crackling of a shorted wire, there blinked a fabulous florescent display - 'The Lonesome Gator Motel'.

Exhausted and weary of his own scent, Mike pulled off the road and up to the front office. Mike suspected the people who owned the cars that were parked outside. Tomorrow, the strangers would probably move on, never looking back. They, at least, had that going for them.

Maybe this wasn't a real motel. Maybe it was just a dingy front. A quick 'in and out' joint for local hookers. Maybe the cars belonged to the owner. Maybe his name was Norman Bates. Mike felt paranoid.

After a few insistent rings at the locked office door, it swung open. Inside the dimly lit interior, Mike saw an old woman who could have easily been the wife of the weird guy from the gas station. She had large watery eyes that peered at him like a bug. Around her throat she had draped a stained, painfully out of style scarf. Her fingertips barely poked out of the over-long sleeves of her cheap polyester jacket-blouse. Her nails were blackish and ungroomed. Without speaking, she motioned Mike inside, her eyes darting about in the darkness outside. She loosened up after the door was re-bolted behind him.

"Want a room?" she asked in a raspy, hushed tone.

"If you've got one," Mike replied sarcastically.

It was starting already. Just as he had imagined. Could it be that every person at Pine Level was a moron? When the asylums were closed, is this where morons set up shop? He forced back the swelling feeling of unease off and hastily scrawled his signature on the water-stained guest register. "MasterCard okay?"

"Sure," she stammered. "Whatever."

She pulled down a key with a dirty, well-handled macrame thong woven through it and handed it to him. "Number four, down at the end. Check out's noon. Key goes through the slot in the door when you leave." Mike put down his credit card and waited while she struggled to make an impression. The ocean smell lingered in the room. "Any restaurants nearby that you'd recommend?"

"Half a mile towards town," she nodded. "The Stumble Inn. Food's not bad, but they ain't open late. No one out this way is open late," she stated.

"Think I have time for a shower?"

Her nose crinkled up. "You better," was all she said.

The shower sprang to life with the force of a leaky faucet, but it was hot and it felt good after a day on the road. The room was clean, Mike thought. Probably the work of some cheap Cuban cleaner. Certainly, the old woman couldn't have done such a fine job herself. She didn't seem to have the wherewithal to even scrape the grime from under her fingernails, let alone do any housekeeping.

Mike dressed as quickly as he could and thirty minutes later, he was walking into the large rough-hewn barn of a place called 'The Stumble Inn'.

It was a relief to see clearly because the light wasn't so dim. A jukebox played CCR's 'Run Through the Jungle' off a scratchy 45 and one drunk fellow danced with himself in the center of a spacious hard-wood floor.

There were some pretty girls. One was a stunning green-eyed temptress with jet black hair, ample breasts, a small strawberry tattoo on her left shoulder and lips that would take a priest's mind off a choir-boy. Her trailer park beauty marred only by a strange, ugly growth that sprouted from her elbow like a craggy fungus. Mike later discovered its name was Ed. Big Ed, of course.

Like most local bars, the customers stared at strangers as they entered, but it didn't get under Mike's skin. He had the same curiosity about them as they did for him, and besides, the food was edible, the service expedient and the drinks stiff. Even backward idiots live well.

No one other than the resident billiard queen, who also doubled as the server, spoke to him, but she was pleasant, if somewhat in a hurry. Everyone appeared to be in a rush. What was eating these people? Mike wondered. They might be edgy, but it wasn't as easy to dismiss as that. They didn't seem fearful of anything tangible, just apprehensive. Any noise from outside was quickly investigated, and no one seemed eager to head for home either. Those that didn't huddle over their drinks literally shouted and laughed as hard as they could to convince themselves that a cloud of fear didn't hang over the place.

Mike caught the raven-haired maiden looking his way a few times, but Big Ed kept an iron grip on her and she didn't stray far. Better that grip stay on her arm than on Mike's neck, he figured. They might meet up again. Maybe Big Ed would have to go fishing or clean his gun or something and Mike could reply to that "fuck-me-stranger" invitation that twinkled deep in those beautiful sea-green eyes.

Ed, for all of his meat-for-brains appearance, had the distinction of being the most feared hulk in the bar. Every joint had one. They come with the liquor license, and he looked for all the world to be a Maytag washer repairman on steroids. Right now, all of his worldly possessions seemed to travel on two shapely legs in ruined nylon stockings. Ed glanced at Mike and almost sneered. He was not an extrovert where strangers were concerned and his quick, hard stare let Mike know he wasn't welcome to belly up at Ed's corner of the pine wood bar.

After a momentary stare-down, Ed's eyes broke away and laughed at some unfunny story that drifted down the bar and returned his attentions to the green goddess with the strawberry tattoo that leaned by his side. Mike refocused his attention on a double shot in a rocks glass and hoped that Big Ed would become so drunk that getting it up later would have more to do with his dinner than his dick.

Suddenly, a faint sound rocked the establishment. It wasn't too far to go unmentioned. It was the echoing pop of gunshots. Four of them. Shotgun by the sound of them. Then nothing. A few men reluctantly ventured outside, but returned quickly without comment.

Even Big Ed seemed edgy in his attempt to brush off the excitement. No one looked eager to leave. Millie, the pool shark waitress, served up another round and Mike wondered if the 'Stumble Inn', which they had informed him always closed early, was going to close at all tonight. They would have to use a crowbar to get them off their stools.

One old patron broke away from his permanent post at the dark end of the bar and staggered back a few steps.

"Jes' like I tol' ya," he barked at the others. "Sure enuff!"

The bartender, pretending to scarcely notice the outburst, whispered under his breath, "Let it go, Charlie."

"You know it's as they say," the old guy stammered.

Mike wanted to ask who "they" were.

The barkeep told them to sit down.

"Like Hell!" the old man shouted. "It took'em long enough, but true is true and y'all know it! You're jest as sceerted as me. Any as says they ain't is a liar. I'll drink with none of ya."

"Then take a hike," snarled Big Ed, rising from his ass-worn bar stool.

The old man staggered back, fearful of the unnatural physical size of Ed. "You think you kin do as you want cuz you's tied in with her," he spoke defiantly, pointing at the green goddess. "But there's no way to keep'em out. Sooner or later... well, you know." The old man tottered towards the front door. He muttered, "You know..." once more before disappearing through the door.

As Mike turned back from watching the old guy's exit, he realized that everyone, absolutely everyone, was staring at him. Hard. Mike felt extremely vulnerable.

"I guess he's had a few too many," Mike said to anyone listening.

"That's about the size of it," agreed the barkeep. "His old lady's about to go into labor."

"Well, then he should go home," Mike offered.

"Yeah, he should," the man replied.

After a silent moment, everyone went back to their pretense of having a good time.

Something strange and creepy was happening in this sleepy little rattrap, Mike thought. Something dark and gnawing. A grim infection that was slowly seeping out of a hidden wound somewhere and poisoning everyone's blood, driving them insane. How long had this quiet madness been going on? Mike couldn't even guess. Veiled or not, he would find out.

Tonight wasn't that night, nor were these the people he wanted to get close to. Once settled, there would be an opportunity to inquire into such secretive things. The patrons of the rustic bar seemed ruffled enough by his mere presence and a few bruisers in there looked like they would enjoy seeing his face rearranged.

Mike finished his dinner of deviled crabs, which were excellent, and fries, which were greasy and tasted of deviled crab, and downed his double scotch and soda under the scrutinizing gaze of the yokels. He paid his check, left a generous tip and walked towards the door feeling like the goddamned bravest man in the place. All eyes were on him as he paused just inside the front door. These guys were petrified.

Without a tremor, he stepped outside and felt an overwhelming urge to scream at the top of his lungs and rush

back inside just to scare the bejesus out of them. He fought
the urge. This was a pretty humorless lot.

Out in the night, everything was still. No ghosts, goblins
or ghouls awaited the unwary beyond the safety of the
hillbilly bar. His car was where he left it and soon he was
back at 'The Lonesome Gator', crawling into the overstuffed
bed and wishing the black tressed goddess with the green
wicked eyes was sprawled naked on top of him.

He wondered what the old fool at the bar was talking
about. It had something to do with Big Ed and his tattooed
girlfriend. Mike wasn't far off the mark in guessing the old
character's concerns were directed towards the stunning
green goddess.

Something was being strongly hinted at, and it was no
secret amongst the denizens of the bar. Mike seemed to be
in the dark, and that, he thought, is how it should be. He
was little more than a stranger who had wandered in from
the night.

Before dozing off, Mike's attention was drawn to an old,
simple needlepoint sampler that was framed on the wall
opposite the bed. He strained to read it in near darkness.

It said "Lest Ye Ever Forget". In the lower right corner was
a date stitched in faded rose thread - 'April 1928'.

# CHAPTER FIVE

— • —

I T WAS JUST BEFORE sunrise on Monday morning, and the sandy expanse of Bonita Bay was still deep in shadow. Waves rolled in, accompanied by a screeching flock of gulls that swung about overhead busily picking up the small fiddler crabs that ran in wild circles beyond the surf, waving their one over-sized claw up towards the sky, almost daring the birds to eat them.

The outsider who came down the beach marred the scene, walking along the surf's edge, fishing gear in hand. Gulls screeched their disapproval and snatched up a few remaining crabs before departing to quieter shores.

Ray Butler always came down to the shore at six a.m. sharp. Every morning. Six a.m. It was his routine. Strictly adhered to.

For years he had labored as a diesel truck mechanic, always taking a certain amount of pride in fixing up an ailing big rig and watching it roll onto the highway and off towards New England, or South Carolina, or wherever big rigs head. More days than not, he wished he was at the wheel himself, commanding the big semi as it left Lakeland far behind.

Days turned into years and Ray moved up in the ranks, becoming indispensable to the overlords of diesel truck repair and he put a little something away for days like this one.

A tiny bungalow and a Ford Ranger pickup were all he required to be content. A few dollars in the bank and a quiet place to fish was all a nine-to-fiver could hope for. Guys like Ray never got rich. They weren't supposed to. Somebody had to be on the front line, the foot soldier, but in a perfect world there was, occasionally, a small reward to be had and this was it.

Ray Butler squinted out to sea. A warm glow met his eyes on the horizon. There was a chill breeze, but that would soon drop away and the temperature would climb to its usual humid 85 degrees, maybe higher.

He enjoyed this time of day the most. The time before the sun really got stoked and those annoying teenagers headed for the sand with their over-sized Bart Simpson beach towels and ear-splitting radios. At this moment of the day, a man could fish quietly, unbothered.

Ray liked to fish and sip a hot bourbon-doused coffee. He'd sit flat on his butt and jerk a sharp barb into the mouth of anything foolish enough to try his bait. He was a retired diesel mechanic, damn it, and casting a line was his sport. It was better than sex; he had often insisted. Well, better than the sex he got, anyway.

Ray surveyed the bay and set his rump down not too far from the jagged rocks that shaped the inlet's southern tip. If he caught anything worth taking home, he didn't have to walk as far. He dropped his towel and pushed it around with his toe.

It was a rotten smelling old towel with more than a smattering of dried fish blood and guts ground into it. After he had prodded it about, he sat on the grimy thing. He laid the rod and reel and other essential gadgets on the towel beside him and struggled to dislodge the cap from his thermos.

He cursed the tightness of the lid as he wrestled it off. The jarring action sending a goodly portion of the scalding liquid across his lap. It burned like hell but smelled terrific.

His next challenge was to see if he could bait the hook without running the barb through his thumb. He reached into the bucket and felt around for one of those live jumbo shrimps he'd bought just before sunup. Getting a grip on one of the slimy bastards was something else. The shrimp don't seem to mind being boiled alive in a pot of beer, but sticking a hook through their back was something else again. Ray cornered one spiny little prospect and got him out of the bucket. He gripped it in his right hand and poised the hook just above the shell near the tail. If inserted just right, the shrimp wouldn't die for a long time and their incessant squirming and wriggling will send their terror-filled vibrations through the water to the intended recipient.

Ray swallowed a long, hot swig of his spiked coffee and watched the impaled shrimp dance a painful jig on the end of his line. It was a weighty little shit; he thought. Why don't they ever serve them this big in restaurants?

He swung the rod back over his shoulder and let the dancing shrimp fly with a powerful cast that sent it flailing far out into the surf. He strained to see where it splashed down, but the sun nudged itself up out of the water and the glare made it impossible to judge the distance. Satisfied that it had, in fact, gone far enough, he gave the shrimp a few swift jerks with the rod. Keep the bait alert, he figured. Make it do its job.

Nothing seemed to happen, so he started slowly reeling the line in towards shore. From time to time, he would let the shrimp quiver for a moment before pulling him in a few more feet. If he reeled it in too quickly, he'd have to cast it back out again.

Ray relaxed. This must be what heaven was like. He reached for his small plastic thermos cup. It was empty. With his free hand, he attempted to unscrew the stubborn cap again, without success. He propped the rod under his arm and applied both hands to the stubborn container and that's when all hell broke loose.

The rod jumped out of Ray's cradling arms. If he hadn't reacted so swiftly, the reel would have disappeared into the surf altogether. He dumped the hot coffee in his lap and struggled quickly to his feet, clutching the rod fiercely. Whatever he had, it was a fighter. Maybe a big snapper, he thought. They have a peculiar type of gyration they go through when hooked.

What else could it be? Ray thought. A big Red Snapper. He smiled and set his jaw for the struggle. Man versus fish. It was the natural order of things.

It lunged about and thrashed for a few minutes before Ray could get it creeping towards shore. The game tired fast. Becoming worn out like all the others before it. Ray kept reeling the line in, but it wasn't easy. Even in its tired, worn-out state, this baby fought like a tiger. Maybe it wasn't a Snapper. Maybe it was something else. Something better, bigger.

Ever since a Blacktip shark had bitten through his line on Walker's Cay, Ray had used a fifteen-inch steel wire leader. Nothing could bite through that. Nothing.

He could pull his prize in no farther. It wasn't budging from its last position some twenty yards out. It circled, darted, and swam about weakly, but it wasn't coming in. Ray's excitement had risen to a peak, and he was prepared to wade into the surf and wrestle his trophy out by hand if need be. He yanked the rod hard one last time before changing tactics.

"Okay," he sneered. "You want to play tough? I'll give you tough!"

He waded into the water, reeling in the slack line as he went. It stretched to where the water was only four feet deep. His aged heart pounded from the effort and his chest pained him, but it was worth it. This baby might even end up on the wall, he guessed. Screwed to a polished wooden plaque with the lucky hook dangling from its gaping mouth.

Ray reached the spot where the line dove taut into the surf. He thought about what might be under the surface for a long moment before thrusting his hand into the surf. He didn't enjoy sticking his hand down where he couldn't see, but this was serious stuff.

"All right, you sonofabitch! It's the fucking barbecue for you!" he snarled. He groped around for a few seconds, searching the cloudy green water for a handhold on his catch. As soon as he touched it, his complexion went grey and his mouth dropped open in a startled expression of confusion and surprise. Something wasn't right. His startled eyes bulged as the water around his arm swirled violently and churned red.

"Jesus Christ!" he screamed, jerking his arm out of the water.

There was nothing left beyond his forearm but a hint of bone and muscle. Followed soon by a torrent of blood. Ray was in shock. He just stared at the empty space where his hand had been moments before. He stumbled back a few feet and mouthed a few unformed words. His eyes never moved from the gushing stump that was once his arm.

In front of him, the water thrashed in a growing whirlpool of gore. Through the churning blood and pink foam, something big moved. The dark shape rose from the shallow water. It broke the surface with its smooth black head until a glittering set of large, opulent eyes appeared. They fixated him. It kept rising until it towered above the terrified man.

The thing sparkled in the orange light of the morning sun. Water trickled down its hide in glistening rivulets that formed tiny streams in the heavy creases of its black skin. It wore the remnants of tattered clothing that seemed out of place on its hideous frame.

As it stretched upward to its full height, Ray saw the teeth. Row upon row of sharp serrated knives, at least four sets on the lower and upper jaws. Four sets, eight in all. Perhaps two hundred rippling blades. Ray couldn't move. Couldn't even think of moving. Couldn't even think.

It sank to his feet like anchors in the sand. The vast mouth opened slightly, vomiting forth a bucketful of sea water out between the fatal saw blades. In its lower peeled back lip hung Ray's new hook, bright and shiny.

Ray saw its eyes twitch. It looked at him curiously. Large, soulless cat's eyes that bulged squarely from the outer edges of its face. When they blinked, the pupils blew open completely, then shrank back rapidly to tiny slits. Ray could see his own reflection in those large, glassy eyes.

It blinked a few times before reaching out a massive, veined claw towards Ray's throat. He watched as it paused for just a beat and then swung an effortless blow at his neck. A blow that split the tender flesh of Ray's throat with scalpel-like efficiency.

Blood and gurgled words poured out of the wound in a crimson flood that soaked his chest. Ray uttered a scream from his severed windpipe. It came out as little more than a blood-wet wheeze. His last conscious sensation was of having his hair tangled in the thing's grip and feeling it give him a quick, powerful snap that broke his vertebrae with a sickening crunch. Salt stung his frozen eyes as Ray, still alive but paralyzed completely, disappeared beneath the swirling blood-stained waters. A few moments passed, and all became calm once more.

On the beach, a few inquiring gulls ventured back to discover Ray's bait bucket full of live jumbo shrimp. The largest bird boldly toppled the bucket onto its side, spilling the contents and scooped up the thrashing shellfish before flying off towards a new adventure.

# CHAPTER SIX

— • —

M ITCH WAS CUTER THAN the average seven-year-old, but Tod despised him anyway. The tyke was short for his age, which made him cuter still. He was not especially keen on socializing with Tod, who Mitch found obnoxious, or his older sister Susan, but he was their prisoner... at least until their folks returned from town.

At least the kid was an annoyance with a fringe benefit, Susan. Mitch wasn't interested in his sister or Tod. He was fascinated by the water's edge and what discovery could be made by poking his fingers into things other people grew sick at the sight of. A collector of rare oceanic oddities, Mitch had a representative museum of the weird growing like a fungus in his family's vacation bungalow.

Susan was nineteen but packed a twenty-one-year-old's bikini to the legal limit. She drew in a slow, deep breath that expanded her chest. The girl exhaled just as slowly. She was a pretty girl whose family came to the bay every summer from nearby Palm City for a quick getaway.

Tod watched with young lust as she strolled out of the surf and dropped onto a faded beach towel beside him. She kept her wet, sand-covered feet off the towel and reclined on one elbow.

"Turn it up," she said, motioning to Tod's oversized radio. "It's too quiet out here."

Tod grinned and gave the already deafening blaster another crank. He looked down the beach to where Mitch was tormenting some slight form of ocean-life that had washed ashore, then returned his attention to Susan. Tod didn't give a damn what the kid was doing. He wanted to stay far away.

Her shoulder length hair was an auburn that competed with her deep tan. When Susan looked out over the incoming waves, her watery blue eyes searched for nothing in particular. Nothing was out there today. Nothing ever was.

Tod bumped her from behind and she let out a low, startled, but predictable, gasp. She felt Tod's hands cupping her young breasts. He massaged them for a few seconds before attempting to guide her onto her back. She resisted, almost spitefully, until she felt her bikini top slipping off. With one swift movement, she rolled over and stared hard into his face.

He wasn't much to look at during the summer. She let his mouth press against hers. It was comical, she thought, but not a bad try for a sophomore. He worked at pushing his tongue between her teeth, but her lips remained as tight as a bear trap. His hand fumbled and poked between the cleavage of her breasts. With surprising luck, he freed one from her bikini. Susan wiggled a bit as the top fell away. A cool breeze of salt air swept over the young tender mounds. Tod felt his heart pounding inside his chest, threatening to explode. He roused a little passion in their kiss and was stroking the soft skin of her uncovered breasts with trembling fingertips. Her modest nipples stood hard and fresh.

Tod's adrenaline-pumped brain, half filled with teenage lust, half filled with terror, implored him to work his way downward and not quiver like an old woman while doing it. He moved, almost trembling, pressing the tip of his tongue against the peak of her breast. He kissed it.

Instantly, the erotic episode slammed to a halt. Susan pushed him off with the skill of a power lifter and sat up straight. She whipped the straps of her bikini onto her shoulders and glanced down the beach.

"Mitch! Where's Mitch?" she asked.

Tod scanned the shoreline. "Who cares?" he shrugged. "He's around here somewhere."

"No!" Susan protested. "I'm supposed to be watching him and I can't do it with my eyes closed."

Tod jumped up, searching the beach for the little trouble-maker. Wishing he could rap his knuckles across the kid's head.

"Isn't that him?" he asked, pointing towards a tiny speck in the distance.

"Yeah, I guess so," she said, straining her eyes.

"Look," Tod said. "He's busy rooting around in that old seaweed and shit, having fun. Leave'em alone." He moved close to her once more and pressed his chin against her bare shoulder. "So could we..."

"I've got to keep him in sight. He's too far away," she insisted. "Mitch! Mitch!," she shouted. "Come back down here!"

She began waving her hands above her head; her breasts jiggling back and forth as only young breasts can. Mitch got the signal and started back. She turned to Tod, satisfied.

"We still have a few minutes," she said, smiling. "But keep your mitts off my tits." With that, she lay back and stretched her arms behind her head, tensing every muscle. Tod just stared out into the Gulf, mesmerized. The glittering water seemed to have a hypnotic effect on him. Susan tugged at his hair until he eased back. She looked up at him and pulled his ears.

"When Mitch gets here, I'm going to send him up to the house. Then we can take a walk," she whispered, pulling his mouth down to hers. This time, her lips were wide open.

It took Mitch ten minutes to cover a five-minute walk. He came back in a slow drag-ass fashion, engrossed by the things he had found on his morning hunt. Ahead, he saw his sister necking with his chief nemesis, the evil Tod. One foot followed the other in a paced march. Mitch looked straight ahead, his eyes fixed on the dry-humping teens. He moved a little more quickly as he approached the entangled couple, staring, pretending not to see. His shadow fell across them, blotting out the sun.

Susan raised herself to one elbow, shielding her eyes with her free hand. She could see his face against the sun.

"Mitch," she said. "What's up buddy?"

Tod looked up also, but Mitch remained silent.

"Yeah, short shit," he chided. "What have you got there?"

Mitch looked down to the treasure the ocean had coughed up. He held it up to his eyes, never lifting his head, then with a sudden mechanical motion he dropped old Ray's bloody head into their laps.

Susan screamed, kicking and squirming in the sand. Tod was like a cockroach on its back. All arms and legs. It took a split second to get the grisly trophy off his stomach, where it rolled to Mitch's feet. The kid smiled. Tod and Susan were being funny.

# CHAPTER SEVEN

—·—

T HINGS WERE ALREADY HAPPENING when Mike Reardon
pulled into the parking lot of Pine Level's Municipal
Building. He was late for his first day of work. Sleeping
hadn't been quite the problem he had imagined, and he
now found himself the object of close unfriendly scrutiny
by some disgruntled locals milling around the few police
cars at the front of the building.

As he got out of the car, he noticed their solemn expres-
sions. Their faces were long, distrustful. Mike nodded to
one old mariner as he passed, but the man just stared and
shuffled to where others like him congregated. Their low
voices held a sense of dread.

"No need to roll out the red carpet," Mike grumbled to
himself. "I'm just the new picture-taker. Say 'cheese!'"

The reception area was not much different. He pushed
his way past a handful of migrant workers clustered around
a pay telephone and leaned across the wooden counter that
divided the room.

"Hi. I'm Michael Reardon," he announced to a mid-
dle-aged woman, identified as Margaret by her name
badge. "I'm the new photographer and microfilm clerk."

She looked at him, unimpressed. "From Miami?" she
sighed.

"Yeah."

"Come along," she said, wagging a finger at him. "They'll
definitely want to see you." She opened a swinging gate
and motioned Mike to step inside. He followed her down

a short hallway, which led past several small offices. When they came to the third open doorway, she gave her head an official snap to the left. Mike took this as some kind of signal to go inside. He flashed the desk lady a smile and sidled past her into the room.

It was brightly lit and cluttered. Towards the back of the office was a large, messy desk with a large, messy man sitting at it. He was on the telephone. Mike had a fair idea that this was Pine Level's Sheriff Robert Lynch, whose name plate peeked out from under a heap of scattered papers. The big man glanced up at Reardon with weary eyes. A faint look of realization and aggravation skimmed across his features. Without interrupting his conversation, he motioned Mike to sit. The only chair was opposite the desk, and on it was a small grease-soaked cardboard tray with the cold remains of fried catfish and hush puppies in it. Mike grinned and brushed the container into an overflowing waste can. Most of the hush-puppy crumbs spilled onto the floor, but he pretended not to notice.

Sheriff Lynch finished chewing out the other end of the line, slammed the phone down hard and glared at Mike. "Where the hell have you been?" he demanded. "I've been on the horn to Miami all goddamn morning!"

"I... I overslept," Mike admitted. "It was quite a drive here last night and the motel didn't give me my wake-up call."

"You ever hear of an alarm clock, kid?"

Mike just sat there feeling vulnerable and stupid.

"Did you bring your camera?" the sheriff asked.

"Back of my car."

"Get it."

Mike stood up and crept towards the door.

"Excuse me," he said, turning back to the big man. "But who exactly are you?"

The man looked annoyed and smiled at Mike from behind his desk. "I'm your new boss, Reardon. Bob Lynch, Sheriff of Pine Level. They call my deputies the 'Lynch Mob'. You'll meet'em, but right now go fetch that camera and meet me in the crime lab."

It impressed Mike. "You've got a Crime Lab?"

"Last door... end of the hall."

Mike hurried out, making a beeline for his car. He got the impression that things weren't as smooth and cozy as they used to be. Maybe those gunshots he heard last night had resulted in a bit of unpleasantness. Maybe a killing. This might explain the dreary looks on the people outside the station. Maybe there was a blood feud going on in the woods between warring hillbilly factions. Real Hatfield and McCoy stuff. Maybe it was escalating.

The townspeople's air of distrust and cautiousness had an unnerving effect. He hurried past the stone-faced citizenry in the parking lot and attempted to raise the trunk of his prized Corvair. It was tighter than a hooker's corset. He looked around. Sure enough, every hick in the lot was staring at him. No opportunity for slick tactics, he reckoned. Time was of the essence. He reared back and gave the trunk a solid kick that sent it flying open with an aching creaakkk. He dove into the back space, digging through the mess of clothes, books, and junk he had brought along on the trip. Somewhere in that tangle, he found his camera.

"They're going to love me around here," Mike snickered. "The natives always worship the guy who takes their picture." He'd seen it in a Tarzan movie.

As he walked, he fiddled with the gear, attaching the flash bar and checking the exposure index of the film. What this was about wasn't clear but from the grave faces outside, but Mike figured it had to be good and nasty. Whatever it turned out to be, he could photograph it.

As he passed by one open doorway, an elderly, digni- fied man stepped out, intercepting him. "Mr. Reardon?" he asked in an officious manner. "The photographer?"

"Yes sir," Mike replied.

"I am Dr. Johann Politzer," he announced, looking at Mike's camera. "I assume you're used to this kind of thing, eh? See it all the time?"

Mike looked at him curiously as they both walked towards the lab. Politzer was tall, not especially thin, with a lined, interesting face that denoted his age and had a distinguished head of silver hair, although his mustache was still quite dark.

"You the local doc?" Mike asked.

"Oh no," Politzer smiled, shaking his head. "Just whiling away the summer here with my wife, Sophia. Local doctor left town a few weeks ago. Took off abruptly without even a hint of where he was going, so I've been helping wherever I can."

"Some vacation," Mike grinned.

"No problem... wife's a bit of a bore, if you know what I mean."

Mike nodded as if he knew something about a bored wife.

"Besides, this has all taken a very interesting, if unfortunate, turn. It's getting very exciting around here, as I'm sure you've already heard." Politzer stopped, showing the door marked 'Crime Lab', and pushed it open, allowing Mike to enter first.

There was a long steel table in the center of the room. On three sides of the work area were steel cabinets that came waist high and housed an assortment of sophisticated equipment, rarely seen outside of a much larger city. Sheriff Lynch stood at one end of the polished examination table, filling out a clipboard overflowing with reports and forms.

Lynch looked up from his work. "Glad you could find it, kid," he said sarcastically. "Now I can stop doing this paper bullshit!" The sheriff looked at Politzer, then at Mike. "I see you've met the doctor. Did he fill you in on this goddamn nonsense?"

"Well, not exactly," Mike said. "But he mentioned it was bordering on the unusual."

"I don't think you're going to like this, kid."

"It's not a matter of liking it, Sheriff," Mike interjected.

"Well, it's your first day, Reardon, and normally I would have cut you a break."

"I don't deserve any breaks, Sheriff," he told the gray-haired lawman.

"Then you ain't likely to get none," Lynch snorted.

Politzer stepped between them, motioning to a covered metal lab tray that sat on a side counter. "I must admit Mr. Reardon," he began, "you seem awfully eager for a man who photographs crime."

"As long as I don't have to take a picture while it's happening, I get by."

Lynch picked up the weighty tray and slid it to the center of the examination table like a fresh roasted turkey. A white, blood-stained hand towel obscured the contents.

Lynch asked the doctor what he found.

Politzer rested his chin on his hand as he shook his head. "Not too much. Everything's about as you remember it."

"Why all the double talk?" Mike asked. "You people are as vague as the 'Stumble Inn' menu."

The Sheriff looked at Reardon for a moment. Maybe there was more gut to this kid than he'd first thought. Lynch could sense Mike's condescending attitude towards Pine Level, its people and him, and he wasn't fond of smart-ass rejects out of Miami, cutting their teeth on his turf either. But maybe there was something more here. Perhaps past the anger and humiliation the kid seemed to harbor, there was something worthwhile. Lurking just underneath.

"Why don't you lift that cover off for me, kid?" Lynch suggested.

"Don't think I won't," Mike said as he grasped the corner of the crimson-soaked cloth. With the flair of a seasoned magician, he tossed it back.

Ray's severed head was staring straight into Mike's face. Their eyes met, sort of. Ray only had one eye. His face was a frozen mask of horror, the lips peeled back in a gruesome, twisted scream. Around the eye sockets, nostrils and mouth, the skin had become puffy and purple white. Blood seeped like syrup in a slow, but steady trickle from the ear canals, forming a puddle in the tray. The infusion of sea water into the tissue caused the head to bloat to a third larger than its normal size. Lynch took a convenient walk to the other side of the room, pretending to search for something.

Politzer looked at Ray's head with a grim fascination. He seemed unaffected by the sight of such a horror. Mike was pale but stared at the head just the same. His eyes traveled down to where Ray's neck ended. It was a clean cut. The bones, arteries and windpipe were severed so quickly that there was no noticeable tearing of the flesh.

"Something very sharp did this," Politzer surmised. "Something sharp and powerful."

"Quick too," Lynch said. "Look at that expression. He was still screaming when it happened. Like a goddamn chainsaw through butter!"

Mike appeared not to be listening. He fumbled with the controls on his camera. He was white, with little chance of taking on any other color.

Politzer looked on with subdued amusement as Mike tried to concentrate on the lump of contorted meat that had been a man's face. He changed his angle slightly in order to include the exposed side of the severed throat, twisting the focus ring, trying to steady his trembling hand.

He held his breath and snapped the first exposure. This gave him the extra boost of courage needed to keep going. He reached forward, touching the corner of the tray. With a little tug, he started turning it towards him for a better angle. As his finger tipped the edge, barely three inches away from Ray's silently screaming blue mouth, Mike saw something move.

A gore-covered crab burst scurrying out of Ray's gaping eye socket, dragging the bloody, slime drenched orb in

one claw as it ran with lightning speed straight up Mike's
out-stretched arm, leaping onto his face.

Somebody crushed the escaping little bandit under their
foot, but Mike didn't know who. In his condition, he didn't
care. He just wanted a drink.

# CHAPTER EIGHT

— · —

O NE SHOT GLASS FELL into place after another as Mike
lined them up in front of him. It wasn't quite the Great
Wall of China yet, but he was working on it. He looked up
from his project and waved to the bartender. "Let's do it
again," he called.

"A man drinks like that, and he don't eat, he's gonna
be sick for sure," said the barkeep, who was the biggest,
blackest Haitian Mike had ever seen.

"Don't you worry about me, pal," Mike grinned. "I ate a
handful of aspirin before I came in."

The Haitian just shook his head and poured another shot
of tequila. "You gonna be sick for sure," he opted.

"No way. I was sick. Now I'm just numb and happy to be
here with you, thanks."

"What made you carry on like that?" asked the Haitian.

Mike smiled weakly, glancing around the small bar once
to tally up the clientele before spilling his guts. The place
was empty despite two cute college types sitting at a back
table. Turning back to the big Haitian, Mike leaned forward
secretively.

"I saw the victim of a shark attack today," he said in a near
whisper. "Let me correct that... I meant to say, I saw the
head of a shark attack victim today."

"Why, I ain't heard of no shark business around here in a
long, long time," the barman said in disbelief.

"Me either," Mike added. "But then, I just got here." His
voice grew a little louder and more animated as he spoke,

attracting the two girls at the back table. They stopped
their conversation and began listening to what Mike was
telling the barman.

"Well, I had to take a picture of this guy's head, right? And
just as I was snapping a real tight close up for the boys back
home, this fucking crab runs out of the guy's eye socket and
jumps in my face!"

"Jesus and Mary!" Nate exclaimed, crossing himself.
"What you do then?"

"Well, I passed out. I think. And when I came to, I was
looking at you," Mike said. "Now, is that bottle empty yet,
or what?"

"Why you takin' pictures of a dead man's head?" Nate
asked, pouring a fresh shot of liquid confidence. "Don't be
tellin' me they's gonna run it in the newspaper."

"Not exactly. Strictly police business. I shoot all the neat
stuff. Came all the way from Miami, too."

"This is far away from where most neat things are happening," he said. "Somebody must'a liked you real good."

"Yeah, somebody liked me real good all right," Mike grunted. "I'll tell you about it sometime. It's one of those stories
that tells better with a few drinks, but mister, while it was
going down, it was heaven."

"Gotta be a woman," the bartender said, pouring himself
a shot. "Gotta be somebody else's woman."

"Amen, brother."

"Once there was a guy got bit by a shark off Lighthouse
Point, damn near took his entire leg off. Had to close the
beach for two solid weeks! Boozin' business was great."

"I'll bet. It must have been news here."

"That it was, sir," answered the Haitian in a low voice.
"That it was."

Mike noticed a shadow on his shoulder as the bartender
spoke. One girl had come up behind him and was reaching
to set her glass on the bar. Mike looked her over, feigning
disinterest. She was tall, brunette, and possessed a full,
sensuous figure.

The barkeep flashed her a broad, toothy smile. "Another round, Miss Nicki?" he asked.

"No thanks, I'm the designated passenger tonight."

Nate looked past her to the other girl and nodded. "I'm glad you worked yourself a ride with Sheila," he said.

Mike moved his seat to get a better look at her. She was every bit the looker her friend Nicki was, only maybe less tanned and a beautiful honey blond. She wore tight denim cutoffs with little rips in them that let her butt peek out and a bikini top with a slashed shirt pulled over it. Mike approved.

"You still at the lab?" Nate asked.

"No, I finished last month. I'm studying on my own now," the girl replied.

Mike decided the only thing missing was his two cents. "What kind of lab were you working at?" he asked.

Nicki eyed him with a cool distaste. "I don't believe they have introduced us, I'm Nicki."

"Forgive my manners, please. I'm Mike Reardon, cop photographer."

"I didn't know there were any crimes around here to photograph," she said.

"Well, I run the microfilm department also," he added. "But I'm thinking of opening a one-hour shop on the side."

"I see," she said. "The lab I worked at is involved in marine biology."

"Marlin Perkins, National Geographic, that sort of thing," Mike said, nodding. "But I don't think I've seen or even heard of it."

"You wouldn't," Nate piped in. "Being new and all."

"Really, how's that?" Mike asked.

"Why, it's up the coast. About five miles north of Lighthouse Point."

"And I came in from the south."

"You go home that way, don't you, Miss Nicki?" the black man asked.

"Tomorrow," she said. "Tonight I'm staying in town."

"Is this lab anywhere near Bonita Bay?" Mike asked.

Nicki looked bothered for a second but recovered. "Why do you ask?"

"A man was killed there this morning, and I was interested in looking at the beach."

Sheila stepped forward and tapped Nicki on the shoulder. "Let's go kid," she said whispered.

"Hell, Bonita Bay is practically neighbors to the marine lab," the bartender exclaimed.

"Yeah?"

"Yes," Nicki agreed nervously. "That's right."

The news aroused Mike's suspicious nature. "You wouldn't be baiting the water near there, would you?"

"No, of course not," Nicki said, shifting about uncomfortably. "I already told you I don't work there anymore."

Sheila nudged her friend, eager to leave.

"That's right, you did. I'm sorry."

"No trouble, Mr. Reardon."

"Is there a chance I could persuade you to direct me to the Bay... personally?" Mike asked. Now Sheila was squirming. "I can give you that ride you were talking about tomorrow," he pushed. "I'm completely safe... member of the squad and everything. Even got this cool badge," he said, flicking out his new leather case. "It's even got that new car smell."

This seemed to make the girls nervous, but Nicki straightened up a little, laughing falsely.

"Yeah, sure," she said. "I'll meet you in front of Nate's Joint in the morning at eight."

"Oooh, that's early, but I'll be here," Mike assured her.

"Try to sober up by then, or maybe they'll end up taking your picture," she said as she turned and walked out with her friend.

Mike kept watching the girl's backsides until they disappeared through the door. Then he returned his attention to the Haitian. "Did she just walk out of here without paying her tab?" he asked.

"Yeah," Nate chuckled. "Never pays... ain't got no money to speak of, but what the hell? She drinks too much to pay for it, anyway. She's been here a long time... pretties' up ma place. Kinda sad, though. Drinks like you... too much."

"Now that's a cheery thought."

The door of the rustic bar creaked open, allowing a burst of chilly night air to rush up the back of Mike's neck.

"Jesus, mate!" he cracked.

"Oh, sorry Reardon," came an even mannered voice behind him.

Mike twisted around to see Dr. Politzer standing just inside the doorway.

"I was passing by and thought I spotted your car out front," he explained. "I wanted to check on you, but you aren't in need of my company."

Mike's eyes darted to the floor, embarrassed. "I'm the one who's sorry doc, I meant nothing by that. I should've looked first and said something stupid later. Have a nightcap with me?"

Politzer eased up a little and walked towards the bar. "Well, perhaps a brandy," he said, surveying the bottles on the shelf. "Do you have apricot?"

"It only comes neat and clean in here, boss. E & J's the house label."

"Then that's how I'll take it," the doctor agreed.

Nate searched around his back counter, coming up with something that resembled a dusty brandy snifter. He wiped it to sparkling clarity and set it in front of the silver-haired gentleman.

"You were in here last week," the bartender said, pouring Politzer's brandy.

"I don't believe so, no," the doctor replied.

"You and two fellas in nice suits... four, five days ago."

"Well, perhaps," Politzer hedged. "I'm uncertain. This place doesn't look familiar."

"You know something, doc," Mike interrupted. "I'll bet this whole gory business is putting the screws to your vacation."

"Perhaps. You can't imagine how terrible I feel about the whole affair. I've never seen so much blood in all my 35 years of medicine. I sent my wife back home a few days ago, you know."

"But you're sticking around?"

"Well, yes, since I retired, I find my home life rather uneventful. At least here I can be of some use until a new doctor arrives to take charge of things."

"What did you say happened to the regular guy?"

"Why he did up and disappeared," blurted Nate excitedly.

"Left town in the middle of the night, they say," Politzer added.

"Some say he was kilt and his house tore all to pieces. But they's nobody, no nothing... just a big mess," explained the black man, his eyes widening in the telling.

"Oh, I seriously doubt he was murdered," the doctor concluded.

"How's that?" Mike asked.

"He didn't have an enemy in the world."

"You know him?"

"Not really, but I had met him. He'd been around for years. A country doctor, you know. I certainly can't imagine why he'd leave after such a long time or where he'd go, but I don't believe he was murdered. No one ever gets murdered around here, Michael," the doctor mused. "It's against the law."

# CHAPTER NINE

— • —

Around midnight, a sharp, creaking sound split the quiet
night as the wind rattled the old wooden sign marked
Fisherman's Cove. The beach it identified was a dark and
lonely one. Mostly unvisited, and at night, deserted. That's
what made it so perfect.

Slightly off the road was a crushed shell area that served
as a makeshift parking lot. Only one car pulled in that night,
its headlights cutting through a thin fog that moved up the
coast and inland. The door featured a colorful emblem of a
merman holding a three-pronged spear in one hand and a
wreath in the other. Under this, the name 'Triton Project'
appeared in bold, official looking script. The door opened
and a shapely foot sat down on the crushed shell. What
followed was every silky inch of Sheila Barton, the girl who
had been in Nate's with Nicki earlier in the evening. She
looked out over the silent, moonlit cove approvingly. It was
a beautiful scene, she thought. Almost as beautiful as she
was.

Sheila walked to the back of her car and unlocked the
trunk. Inside was a large square box and some small gar-
dening tools. She hefted the box to her shoulder and started down toward the beach.

She was worried about the prying nature Mike had exhib-
ited at the bar and was relieved Nicki no longer worked at
the Triton Project. Sheila hoped Mike was merely making
small talk as a way of introducing himself to her pretty,
young friend. Nicki could use some romantic distraction in

her life, Sheila figured. It might give her something else to think about.

She was happy to leave the lab tonight. Far from the scrutinizing gaze of Sylvia and Gail. They didn't appreciate the fact that she and Nicki were still friends. They didn't like her fraternizing with her either. Sheila knew why. They were jealous. Sylvia lusted after Nicki, or at least she lusted after Nicki's girlish body. Gail was glad the see Nicki go. The relationship was just getting too complicated and after that one singular night when Sylvia got Nicki drunk and Gail came in and found them... well; it felt good to be away from the lab tonight.

Sheila knew she was the odd man out now, especially since Stephen went away. He was the only man who ever worked in the lab, and then only part time. He never suspected the fun and games the tyrannical Sylvia put her charges through but having him around had made Sheila and Nicki feel a little more comfortable and secure. Now he was gone and the sexual tension at Triton Project was thick and oppressive.

As she walked, her eyes searched the desolate beach. She was looking for something in the moonlight, something large and of no ordinary shape. There was one, she thought, walking to a small mound of sand. She lowered the box next to the sand heap and picked up one tool. With a slow, cautious movement, she prodded the little shovel into the soft mound and began removing the sand. She dug down deeper and deeper, without success. This one was a bust, she determined, sitting back on her well-formed haunches. She scanned the beach again. There was another mound not too far away. With a sigh, she climbed to her feet and moved on.

A little digging in this heap produced the desired results quickly. Her face lit up as her hand emerged from the sand, holding a pale, white object that resembled a ping-pong ball. This was what she was looking for. The mound was rich in turtle eggs. Egg after egg was lovingly withdrawn and deposited into the cube shaped box until it was nearly half full.

When Sheila removed the last egg, she dropped onto the sand, exhausted. The digging was hard laborious work, but it paid off. She pulled her loose-fitting shirt off and wiped away the thin layer of perspiration that had gathered on her forehead and between her breasts. The night was misty and warm. Perfect for a swim. Draping the shirt over the eggs, she waded into the surf.

The water felt great after she had done her job. It swirled around her and tickled her inner thighs as she kicked slowly away from the shore. She back stroked out about fifty yards before submerging her head completely. Her face broke the surface gracefully, the honey blonde hair streaming out behind her like a delicate silk scarf. Too bad Nicki wasn't here, she thought. Nicki loved to swim naked.

Sheila's daydreaming was cut short by a splashing sound somewhere to her left. She looked around but saw nothing. She heard it again, this time to the right. Fish jump out of the water, she knew, when they were leaping in terror. In a moment, all was quiet again. Then she saw it. A fin, knife-like in appearance, large and black, circling behind her.

A shudder of terror surged through her as she realized a shark had smelled her presence and was now stalking her. The dorsal fin showed the beast was at least eight feet long and its circling movement left no question whether or not it was aware of her. She tried to suppress her overpowering urge to swim frantically towards shore. She realized that such rapid, panic-induced vibrations could almost certainly ensure an attack of such savageness that survival would be out of the question. Instead, she tried to work her way in, making no sudden movements. She might control her actions, but nothing would stop the terror-charged beating of her heart. She moved. It moved.

She prayed it would linger back long enough to allow her to get to the shallows. Sheila kept swimming in a calm, unhurried manner, keeping her eyes frozen on the jutting fin that trailed her in an irregular, cruising pattern. She sensed the beach was getting closer without even looking at it, and she fought off the gnawing urge to panic and splash madly towards the shore and safety. She seemed to retreat successfully from the creature as the fin dropped farther and farther back, disappearing completely. Suddenly, her knee struck something soft. Sand. She had reached the shore and was in water no deeper than three feet.

Sheila gasped out loud for the first time since she'd seen the shark's fin. Thank God, she thought, standing up. She was now free to tremble fiercely, her body shaking with all the horror she had fought so hard to hold inside. She walked forward on unstable legs, pausing just out of the water to turn, eyes searching, back to the surf.

It was there. Behind her, standing eight feet tall. Black, shiny, the tatters of a shirt hanging loosely from its huge shoulders, a large dorsal fin jutting grossly from its mis-shaped spine. Sheila stared, paralyzed, into its wide gaping mouth. She couldn't move.

As it stared at her, something was moving through the thing's brain. It reached out towards her with its large, clawed hand, but it didn't strike. Razor sharp nails rested against the soft flesh of her shoulder, stroking it, testing it. The thing looked into Sheila's fear struck eyes with a glimmer of understanding... of recognition.

Then it bit into her head.

# CHAPTER TEN

— · —

T HE DREAM ALWAYS BEGAN in the same way: the copter circled slowly, hovering over the lush green tangle that whipped about furiously on the ground below. Jungle brush parted grudgingly to permit the copter to land, and as the blades slowed, the vegetation crept forward once again to reclaim its dominance over the land.

The copter door slid open and a hand-carved briar wood pipe emerged, tapping itself gently against the outer door until the dead ash fell from its bowl. The pipe continued outward until its holder, Captain Donald G. Jackson, could put his foot firmly on the smoldering jungle floor. It was a different kind of smoke.

Captain Jackson surveyed the village from his vantage point of safety near the copter, reluctant to step forward and become involved in the wreckage that surrounded him. Everything had burned to the ground. In fact, if it didn't still move, it was smoldering. Huts, vehicles, animals, and people lay charred all around what had been a peaceful little village in the heart of Viet Nam. It was late afternoon. 1971.

The few remaining soldiers of the original squad that could still move on their own power limped towards the approaching medical helicopters that were now coming down fifty yards farther out, where the field afforded them easier access. Jackson watched as the human wreckage ran, crawled, or were carried to their last hope of escape. The sight of young American boys in such a state sickened

Jackson. He looked over the village once more. Alongside it ran a lazy river that provided fresh water and beyond that were fruited trees. If it wasn't Nam and burnt to a cinder, it might have made a nice postcard.

Even amid such chaos and carnage, Captain Jackson knew there was still a greater danger in the village. From what he had been told, there were at least twenty-five GIs and villagers still alive that needed either medical aid or complete evacuation. That would take time and Captain Jackson's task was to buy them that time. Jackson was a bomb squad man.

When no one seemed to tumble to his presence, Jackson resigned himself to stuffing his still warm pipe into his jacket pocket and leaving the comforting presence of the helicopter. He walked through the blackened bodies and still flaming chunks of God-knows-what, looking for someone who could help him.

Somewhere in the village was an undetonated hand-launched missile. Something that still presented an incredible danger to the already beaten troops.

All around him lay the wounded and the dying. The hopeful and the lost. He might save those that still had a chance. Two young soldiers came by, toting a stretcher with an unconscious officer on it. Captain Jackson reached out a hand to stop them.

"Hold it, men," Jackson ordered, but not too stern.

"Captain?" one boy asked, burdened by the weight of the stretcher. His own arm showing blood above the elbow.

"There's a live missile in this village, and I mean to find it and disarm it. Do you know where it is?" he inquired.

The two boys looked at each other. Fear still bled from their eyes. The one with the name McGee stenciled above his pocket, swallowed hard. "Down by the river," he said haltingly. "That's where it all began."

Captain Jackson nodded, even though he didn't have a clue. These boys were walking in shock. "Thanks, soldier. Now get this man to the medevac," he said. "And see to that arm, son. It might be worse than it looks." The boys took off without further words and Jackson looked towards the river. Infection breeds quickly in a jungle. It seeps into your brain, into your soul, Jackson thought. He wondered where Sergeant George was. He had reported the missile incident and admitted that he couldn't elaborate other than that it was extremely urgent.

Jackson knew it would be severe, but things had concluded except for the undetonated warhead. From what he could see around him the engagement had been a fierce one.

The burned bodies showed signs of great violence having been savaged upon them prior to death. Limbs detached, heads separated from their bodies and worse. Some great battle had taken place here. The only thing missing was the enemy. Among the cinders were a smattering of American GIs and more than a few villagers, but nowhere could Jackson identify any Viet Cong fighters. Even the charred weapons which lay bent and twisted, seemed to show that surprise had taken the soldiers or, and this bothered Jackson most, there had been no encounter with the enemy at all. If that were the case, as all things showed, then what the hell happened? If there was no firefight, how did the missile get fired?

The overpowering stench of death drove Jackson back into motion. The soldiers said the missile was by the river, so he that's where he would go. He retrieved his kit from the copter, instructing the pilot to hold tight and wait for him. He wasn't sure if he could disarm the missile or whether he would have to detonate it by remote control. Either way, it was never a straightforward job. It was the task that helped create stomach ulcers, shaky hands, a drinking habit you could set a watch by and a firm belief in God Almighty. First bomb, last bomb; each one cinched Jackson's gut into a knot until the danger was past, but he didn't care. That knot had become his best friend. If that fist ever left its resting place in his gut, he knew he'd be dead.

He never married, never dared to. Sometimes in his thirty-eight years it had tempted him, but the army was too much of a widow-maker to suit him. He'd thought of marriage — perhaps when he retired if the job didn't retire him first.

Down at the river, he saw the water flowing more rapidly than expected. That was a good sign. Maybe the dead that festered on its banks would not poison it.

His eyes scanned the water's edge. It was not a large missile. If Sergeant George's details were accurate, it shouldn't be much bigger than a large shell casing. North of him, Jackson saw the butt-end of the missile protruding from the brush that hugged the water's edge. How in the hell had it gotten into such a position? Jackson thought he would have to wade into the river to get to it. Not an ideal situation to be forced into if one needed to run like the devil, and there were leeches everywhere, eager to attach themselves to your legs. It was just another of the sickening highlight of the tour.

A heavy sigh of resignation escaped from his lips as he fished in his pocket for his pipe. He didn't dare light it, of course, but the hard stem felt comforting clenched between his teeth. It kept them from chattering.

The water was icy as it sloshed down into his boots. He cursed to himself. It had taken a month to get the boots to where they were comfortable. Now they were bound to stiffen, shrink and smell. His pissed-off attitude provided a nice smokescreen for the rising tension in his gut. Every expletive he knew slithered through his thoughts as he rounded the brush and saw the missile and the thing it was embedded in.

Half in the water, half out it lay. Large, heavy and alien-looking, Jackson thought. It resembled those carved wooden monsters the Cong called 'Gods' and sold in town for a pack of cigarettes. Only this one had been alive. Where it lay on its back, Jackson could see the missile protruding lethally from the chest. They had fired the weapon at pretty close range and while it had failed to pass through the creature and explode, it killed it. Well, why not, Jackson pondered. It didn't have to explode to do its job. The creature was dead, and the missile seemed undamaged. Jackson studied it, the smell of the dead beast curling through what nostril hair he had left. Its claws were stained with the blood of a dozen good men.

Easy pickings, he thought, trying to make his shivering nerve endings settle down. Cut a few wires and get his ass back to the helicopter. If ever there was a walk-away, this was it. He only wished he'd had a camera to take a picture of whatever the large, hideous thing was. Who would ever believe him? He wondered if this was, in fact, the cause of the battle that lay smoldering in the remnants of the village. Could this thing have come out of the river and destroyed an entire squad of trained soldiers? In one last desperate effort, had some brave soldier fired a rocket into its chest and stopped its killing rampage? The stories survivors had to tell would be interesting.

Jackson slowly removed the back of the casing, pausing on and off to look at the black, glistening face of the creature, its eyes fish-like, staring, its rippling waves of razor-sharp teeth slick with human blood.

Jackson could see the wires coming through the mechanism, like twisted veins. He pulled out his cutters, being careful not to touch the dead creature for fear of jarring the missile. He reached in and placed the cutters between the colored veins that were of no interest to him and searched for an accessible angle to the hot one.

The sun was sinking over the jungle and the air was growing cool, but Captain D.G. Jackson was perspiring. The chilly sweat ran down his wrist and dropped like dew on the leathery hide of the dead thing beneath him. Just don't get the wires crossed, he prayed. His hand steadied, and the cutters squeezed down, biting into the red plastic that encased the hot wire. Jackson held his breath for a long beat and snipped the wire. He withdrew his hand and exhaled. His left hand wiped his damp brow and his right hand grabbed the pipe from between his frozen jaws. It was done.

He put the snips in his kit and went back into the river. Suddenly, the creature's claw lashed out and seized him by the leg and thigh. Jackson's blood sailed outward like the spray from a fountain.

Jackson gasped, falling back into the river. He panicked as the cold water poured into his open mouth and felt his head swim as fear and pain swept over his entire body. Then he woke up in a cold sweat.

The dream was always the same.

Captain D.G. Jackson looked around the darkened bedroom. It was just as it had been when he dosed off after the 11 o'clock news. Beside him lay Jessica, the woman he had wed after an engagement of five years. She didn't stir as he bolted upright. She never did. After thirteen years, she had gotten used to his 'peculiarities'. She even slept with earplugs.

Jackson lay down again and stared at the ceiling for a long time. He was now a colonel. He lived in Washington and he didn't diffuse bombs anymore. Now he was a monster hunter. During the day, he tracked them and killed them. During the night, in his dreams, he ran in terror.

# CHAPTER ELEVEN

— . —

A T 8 A.M. MIKE'S rattletrap Corvair pulled into the parking lot of Nate's Joint. Nicki was waiting out front as promised. She was leaning against a rusted iron pipe that precariously supported the beaten sign above the front door. The girl wore a black bikini top and tight jeans and on one shoulder balanced a large canvas tote bag. She was entertaining a group of seagulls with bread. One of the screeching birds darted down toward her, boldly snatching a morsel from her outstretched hand. She smiled when she saw Mike drive up.

Mike asked, "How do you like that? First time in my life I've ever been on time for anything."

Nicki tossed the remaining crusts into the air and walked over to his heap.

"Is this your car?"

"I never said I was rich."

"Won't the Sheriff give you anything better to drive around in?" she said with disbelief.

"Hey, come on," Mike protested. "Listen to that engine purr." The car rattled noisily as if in answer to Mike's challenge. "Well, it got me here from Miami."

"I hope you're not planning to make the trip back soon," she said, climbing in.

Mike looked depressed. "Not for six months, anyway," he replied.

Nicki looked at his long face, finding him attractive. "Let's go," she said.

Mike smiled weakly and revved the engine a bit. "Point the way," he said, flooring the accelerator.

"North."

They took the road up through the sheltering pine forests that bordered the coast for about ten miles. Mike had the top down on the convertible war wagon, and the trip gained a pleasant feeling after a few miles. The wind whipped Nicki's hair, but she didn't seem to mind. Mike was in a constant bother about his own coif, brushing his hair back out of his eyes, wishing to remain as suave as possible.

As they drove, he sensed Nicki loosening up a little. It was hard to talk over the grinding of the car, but he thought he might say something.

"So you're a college student or something like that?" he shouted.

"Yeah," she replied, shouting. "Something like that."

"You a local?"

"No. I came here about a year and a half ago from Clearwater."

"Isn't that where all the old folks go to die?"

"Yeah, Clearwater. St. Pete. I like it a lot better around here," she yelled. "What brings a slick, urban guy like you out to Pine Level?"

"I screwed up in Miami," he said with a inspired grin. "And this is my punishment."

"What'd you do? Take an inappropriate picture of somebody's wife?"

"Worse than that, I took an inappropriate weekend with somebody's wife. Only I didn't know exactly whose wife it was."

"I gather you found out pretty quick."

"No, he let me go for a while, finally lowering the boom on graduation night."

An open space on the side of the road was approaching. A state erected sign announced the area as Bonita Bay.

"Turn here," she said, pointing toward the sign.

Mike gave the wheel a sharp jerk to the left, and the Corvair responded, taking the vehicle onto a gravel road that curved through the hovering trees. Within moments, they were at the end of the trail and facing the gulf.

Mike stopped the car and turned the engine off. Before them stretched the windswept beach, barren and moody.

"This was once a very popular place," Nicki informed him.

"Yeah, it's a great place to get killed," Mike whispered. "What made you decide to move to this area?"

"I got a job through school at the marine lab here. I liked the idea of living by the ocean and just sort of hung around after my money ran out."

"What do you do now?" he asked, turning to face her.

"I dive a lot and collect specimens. I sell them to other labs."

"Self-employed?"

"I like it that way."

Mike took a deep breath and surveyed the beach again. "Let's take a walk," he said, opening his car door.

Finding the door on her side of the car frozen shut, Nicki climbed out over the back and started walking towards the beach. She turned as she walked. "You want to take my picture?" she asked, smiling.

"Sure," he said, pulling his camera out of the bag. "Let me get a light reading."

Nicki walked over to a large rock and leaned back against it. She drew one knee up, resting her foot on the craggy surface, and brushed her dark hair away from her face.

Mike looked through the lens of the camera. "You're beautiful," he said, almost to himself.

"Oh, yeah?" she said in mock astonishment.

"I guess that's an old one."

"I can handle a compliment, but it would mean more if you didn't take pictures of stiffs for a living."

Mike clicked off three exposures in rapid succession. "Is this Bonita Bay?" he asked, pointing. "This entire area?"

"As far as you can see. Fisherman's Cove is that way," she pointed.

Mike snapped off a few shots of the beach area for the files they were building at headquarters. "Anything worth seeing there?"

"That's where the turtles come ashore to lay their eggs," she replied.

"Hey, why didn't you say so? Now there's something worth seeing."

"They only come in at night, but we can walk down there." She took Mike's hand and pulled him in the Cove's direction and, without hesitation, he followed.

They walked for a while until they reached a high rock jetty. "We have to climb to get there. It's on the other side," she explained.

"I didn't know this was going to be work," Mike said. "This is taking out all the fun."

Hand in hand, they crawled over the jagged piles of sea-etched rock until they had gone almost twenty feet straight up the jetty face. From the top, he could see Fisherman's Cove opening up before them. It was a peaceful looking little inlet, ringed with pine and mangroves. It was a small paradise on an unfriendly coast where the water rolled ashore with a gentleness unknown to the surrounding bay areas.

After a breathless moment of silent observance, they edged down the steep decline toward the white sunbathed shore. Mike's brain pounded in his head as he struggled down the cliff-face. He wondered if Nicki had a hangover too. Nate was right about his drinking too much, but Nicki didn't seem bothered at all. Maybe she was more used to it than he had imagined.

"Look there," Nicki said, pointing at something on the beach.

They walked towards the object that lay abandoned in the sand. It was a square box with a shirt draped over it. Mike picked up the clothing, inspecting it.

"Looks like somebody forgot their duds," he said. On the shirt was the image of a pelican encircled by a life preserver. The box had the words 'Triton Project' displayed in bold, red letters on its side. It was full of smashed, half-devoured turtle eggs. Their noses curled at the wretched smell. Mike saw Nicki's interest in the shirt and handed it to her. She turned it in her hands a few times. It was stiff with dried blood..

"This is Sheila's," she said.

"The girl from the bar yesterday? Are you sure?"

"Of course. I gave it to her. It's from my old high school."

"What's her connection with this Triton Project?" he asked, nodding towards the box.

"She works there. It's where we met. That's the lab I was telling you about."

"Does this make sense to you, Nicki?"

"Some of the marine specimens in the lab are fed eggs as supplements. We dig them up when our supplies run low."

"What about the shirt and the blood? This cloth isn't damaged, but the eggs are trashed."

"I don't know. It doesn't seem like something Sheila would do."

"Maybe she cut her hand while digging and took off for help. This tool looks pretty sharp," he said, holding up the digging claw next to the box. "Any dog could have gotten into these eggs."

"I can't help but be worried. Something seems weird about this."

"Is the lab far from here?"

"Just a few miles."

"And you're afraid something bad has happened?"

"After that man died near here, I guess I am concerned."

"Well, come on then," he said. "I'll drive you over there and we can check in on her."

"Thanks, Mike."

As Nicki walked away, he took a few quick snapshots of the box and blood-stained shirt. Before leaving, he wrapped the bloody cloth around one of the undamaged eggs and stuffed it in his camera bag. Mike ran to catch up with the sullen girl.

It was a beautiful, sunny day.

# CHAPTER TWELVE

—·—

I T TOOK ONLY A few minutes to reach the winding road that branched off the main highway and led seaward towards the marine lab. The gravel trail seemed unused, with clumps of brush growing in its center. Mike maneuvered the car around the larger clumps of vegetation and ducked his head as they passed under moss-laden tree branches that hung low across their path in great numbers.

He could see the outline of a large block building through the open spaces in the trees. A monolith of technology, cold and unfriendly. He detected no attempt at a pleasing design in its construction. It was purposeful and sterile. Impossible to warm up to.

The Corvair crept up to the structure with the subtleness of a roaring beast. It coughed, choked, and wheezed itself to a merciful death as Mike popped the key back and pulled it from the ignition.

"Boy, they sure don't make'em like that anymore," he said, patting the dashboard affectionately, but Nicki wasn't laughing. Aside from her concern for her friend Sheila, Mike sensed an uneasy mood at the mere presence of the imposing windowless structure with the title 'Triton Project' emblazoned above the door.

Nicki climbed out, looking for some sign of life. She paid particular attention to the low-lying bushes that ran across the front and sides of the modern fortress. She listened for a long moment, then clapped her hands loudly.

"Michelob! Michelob!" she shouted.

"Make that two," Mike joked.

"Michelob is our dog. He likes beer, but he's a good boy."

They both scanned the ground around the lab entrance, but there was no sign of the pooch.

"Maybe he's inside. Is he housebroken?"

"He could be in there," Nicki guessed. "But it's not likely. Sylvia never liked him very much."

"Now who's Sylvia?" Mike asked.

"You'll see. Come on."

Something far more sinister was going on deep inside the building. Sylvia Trent and Gail Anders were busy with their latest experiment. Behind a large door, they were torturing a spider monkey. The room echoed with the eerie chattering of the caged primate, while the two women calmly took notes. They expressed little compassion for their unwilling captive.

"He's not responding well to the treatment," Gail noted, without looking up from her logbook.

Sylvia shined the flashlight into the monkey's eyes. It screamed at her defiantly.

"It's been three days. We should've seen something by now," she said.

"'He has a greater resistance than the others. Perhaps it's his genetic resemblance to man that has caused a retardation in the sequence," Gail offered, looking at the hostile little creature. "If only he could talk... maybe he'd tell us what he's feeling."

"I'd hate to listen to what that little bastard has got to say to me," Sylvia smirked.

A loud buzzer sounded in the lab. Loud and grating. It sent the monkey into raging fits. Gail and Sylvia exchanged furtive looks.

"Someone's at the door," Gail said nervously.

"Can't be the Avon lady," Sylvia kidded. "Try the intercom."

Gail approached the control box on the wall next to the lab door. She pressed the large button. "Who is it?" she asked.

"It's me, Nicki," came the filtered voice over the box.

Gail waited a long time before speaking. "Okay, I'll be out in a few minutes."

Nicki and Mike stood in a small lobby area facing an intercom the size of a telephone book.

"They're probably in the quarantine lab, so it'll take a few minutes for someone to get here," she said.

"What's in there?"

Nicki's eyes shifted about uneasily. "Classified experiments mostly," she replied. "Nothing interesting, really"

"Anything dangerous?"

"No, why do you ask?"

"Just curious," Mike said with a shrug.

Gail left the room after placing the jabbering monkey back in its cage. She took the long walk that wound down many a twisting corridor. It was like a maze; the depth of the multi-level lab being extremely deceptive. Finally, she approached a large door that was ringed with complicated looking switches and levers. With little effort, she quickly pushed buttons and threw switches, and after a good thirty seconds of maneuvering, the immense door swung open. Mike and Nicki were waiting on the other side.

"Nicki you've come back." Gail said. She rushed up to the statuesque brunette, flinging her arms around her neck in a show of mock sincerity.

"It's only a visit," Nicki said with a forced coolness.

Gail backed off a little, noticing Mike. He waved sheepishly, a little ill at ease.

"Who's this?" she asked.

"His name's Mike, he's a photographer."

Mike held his camera up. Gail had a piercing stare, and she was using it on him now. She was obviously suspicious of him and his association with Nicki.

"Can he talk?"

"Like a parrot," Mike piped up.

Gail glared at him and then back at Nicki. She didn't like him being here and wasn't making any attempt to disguise the fact.

"Can we come in?" Nicki asked.

"Where are my manners? Of course," Gail replied. "I've been working a little too hard lately, I guess." She stepped back, allowing Nicki and Mike to enter. He watched as she quickly bolted the door behind them.

"It's a pleasant surprise to see you again," said the voice. Nicki turned to see Sylvia standing at the back of the room. "I figured you were finished with us."

"I just thought I'd stop by and show you something interesting we found on the beach this morning."

Mike watched this tense little drama with rapt fascination. Gail and Sylvia both seemed to undress Nicki with their eyes. He hoped it wasn't a mutual thing. The women looked at her body hungrily and seemed to dislike people of Mike's gender. Too bad, he thought. These girls could thrill a lot of sailors, but they were cold as seawater.

"What do you have?" Gail asked nonchalantly.

"This," Nicki said, pulling the shirt from Mike's camera bag. "It's Sheila's."

Both women registered a mild bit of surprise but recovered quickly. Sylvia was first to step forward, plucking the bundled material from Nicki's fingers. She eyed it closely for a moment, then handed it to Gail. "No doubt the victim of a romantic interlude," Sylvia mused.

"I don't think so, that's blood," Nicki stated bluntly.

"Well, all right... what do you think it means?"

"There was a shark attack off the beach yesterday," Mike said, taking the shirt back from Gail. "And there's blood on this."

Gail gave Sylvia a sideways glance. "Mister....?"

"Reardon... Mike Reardon."

"Mr. Reardon, there is always the chance of a shark attack in any ocean-side community." Gail waved her hand about casually. "This," she continued, "does not mean a shark has eaten Sheila Barton."

"True," Nicki jumped in. "But I found her gear abandoned and became worried."

"That's very noble of you, Nicki, but Sheila is not really missing... officially," Sylvia reminded her. "She'll turn up when she's ready."

As they bantered, Mike let his eyes wander around the barren lobby. Little effort went into putting up a front here. The room was absent of chairs, desks or anything else. It was, in fact, empty except for a square box sitting on the floor.

"What kind of top-secret scientific stuff goes on around here, anyway?" Mike asked.

Sylvia tore her stare away from Nicki and stabbed it into Mike. "I'm sure Nicki must have filled you in on that already, Mr. Reardon," Sylvia replied coldly.

Mike looked at her with an equal coolness. "Sure. I just wanted to hear it from you."

"We study various forms of sea life... plants and animals, to determine how they might best serve mankind."

"Sounds like a man-sized job."

Sylvia winced at Mike's remark and stiffened her spine. The motion made her firm breasts jut out from her shirt like deadly weapons. Mike thought she was going to slap him.

"Where's Stephen?" Nicki asked.

Silence fell over the room.

"Stephen Drake?" Sylvia repeated idly.

"Yes, Sheila said he was gone."

"He moved back to New York about two weeks ago." Sylvia replied.

"Funny, he didn't call me," Nicki said.

"I believe there were personal problems involved. His mother, I think. He was very depressed," Gail interjected. "I'm sure his mind was elsewhere."

"And Michelob?" Nicki asked.

"Did he move back to New York too?" Mike asked sarcastically.

"No, he ran away," Gail answered sharply.

"So, what goes on back there?" he asked, pointing toward the large rubber-sealed doors.

"Very boring... highly classified research," Sylvia replied.

"Can I see?"

"No, I'm afraid not. As Nicki will tell you, the atmosphere inside the lab is very precise, and it is difficult and time consuming to maneuver the polyphonic locks."

"Easy to get in, hard to get out," Mike guessed.

"Exactly."

"Another time perhaps?"

"Maybe."

"You'll have to excuse us," Gail interrupted. "We've got mountains of work to do."

Nicki started backing away, tugging at Mike's elbow. "We understand." Sylvia ushered them towards the door, unbolting it.

"Come back when you can stay longer," she said with a wry twist of her lip. Nicki nodded her head, but her eyes were saying 'no thanks'.

As Mike turned, he saw the box on the floor near the sealed door. There was a rag hung over it, but he could still see its contents. They were small, white orbs. Turtle eggs, to be exact, just like the ones found crushed on the beach.

"What do you do with those?" he asked, pointing down at the box.

"We feed them to our specimens... they're high in protein," Gail replied.

"That's what I thought."

"Women are so predictable," Sylvia grimaced.

Mike and Nicki walked out into the sunlight, glad to be away from the icy sterility of the building. Nicki climbed into the car and stared ahead. Mike thought of drumming up a conversation but opted for a quiet ride back instead. He could sense an inner battle raging inside the young girl but couldn't find the means to combat it. He revved the engine and spun out onto the main road for the return trip.

# Chapter Thirteen

—•—

T HE REST OF THE afternoon was dull. Mike dropped Nicki back off at Nate's Joint and drove over to the Municipal Building. There he went about the business of developing his photographs. The darkroom wasn't new by any means, but it was cool compared to the heat outside and amply stocked. The red light strained his eyes, and the chemicals curled his nostrils. He staggered back to his desk after completing his work.

To kill the boring hours until his shift ended, he pretended to look over the photographs. It was then that he noted the dug-in grooves that ran down the sides of the Triton Project box they'd found earlier. He also noticed Sheila's garden tool a few feet away and figured this must have made the deep gouges.

"Eventful day, Mister Reardon?" came a voice from behind.

Mike swiveled in his chair to see Dr. Politzer standing in the doorway.

"Not really, just trying to stay busy," Mike replied.

"May I?" Politzer asked, holding out his hand for the photos.

"Careful. They're still wet."

Politzer shuffled through the short stack of 8 x 10s, looking at a few with passing interest. "Bonita Bay?" he asked.

"Yes, that and Fisherman's Cove."

"Fisherman's Cove," Politzer said under his breath. "That's near to my place."

"I don't suppose you'd be foolish enough to go swimming, Doc."

"Oh no. Not me," Politzer replied, snapping out of his concentrated study. "You wouldn't want to go splashing about that area now."

Mike agreed and went back to labeling the photographs. Politzer watched him for a few minutes. Becoming bored, he wandered off in search of something better.

Reardon leaned back in his chair when the logging procedure finished and daydreamed about the worried girl he knew that morning. He dug into his pocket, retrieving the scrap of paper with Nicki's phone number on it and, after some hesitation, called her up.

She was still moody, but after some coaxing, Nicki agreed to have dinner. Mike was determined to raise her spirits and some quality time with him was a good a place to start.

Mike took off early since the Sheriff was out. He drove to the Lonesome Gator, where he tried to unpack again. This ritual was one that he undertook daily, never quite making a successful go of it. He would get down about halfway through the stuffed bag and then become distracted. Tonight, that distraction's name was Nicki.

Giving up the task once he found his clean pants, he decided a shower would put him back in proper order. He stepped into the hot spray, directing it on top of his head. It did little more than wash the sand from his hair. Soon, he would have to find a more permanent place to live. The thought depressed him. If only his tenure at Pine Level could be a quick one.

Nicki, likewise, had trouble getting her thoughts straightened out, but they were far more complicated. She calculated and theorized the situation, but it kept coming up in riddles. What had become of Sheila? Did the dog Michelob really run off? Sylvia always hated him? And Stephen? She could ask these questions all night if she wanted. Usually she drank her problems to the mat for a three count, but tonight would be different. Tonight someone would be there for her, to help fill the void and blot out the world.

Nicki had hoped that such a person would come along. Someone with strength, who could face up to trouble without fear. Someone who knew how to stand their ground. For such a person, she would do anything.

She brushed her hair slowly, eyeing her nude body in the dressing-table mirror. Her breasts were full and firm and browned from the sun. She caressed them softly, making her large nipples tighten. It had been ages since she'd looked at them as anything other than excess baggage. Now she wondered what it would be like if Mike was kissing them. Nicki pinched one of her nipples and imagined what Mike's teeth would feel like on them. She pushed this thought out of her head. She had already learned not to expect too much out of life. Just let things happen as they will; it was useless to create happiness or well-being.

She stood up, her hair tumbling seductively over her shoulders as she walked to the closet. She had only one dress, and it was blue. Simple, but it looked new. Nicki had only worn it once before when she interviewed for the position at the Triton Project Lab. She remembered how Sylvia had looked at her, how jealous Gail had become. She tried to push those memories out of her mind. A nightmare had followed that fateful interview. One that was still alive and haunting her, threatening her. She had to push the memory of it out of her brain. Tonight was not the night to remember the shame and humiliation that plagued her from within like a scarlet brand. A drink would help, but no, she was determined to make it through one day without it. She wondered if Mike would help. Could he help? She waited. Lonely. Blue and beautiful. Staring out the window, wishing his car lights would come and save her from the darkness before it was too late.

After what seemed like ages, the lights fell upon her house.

It was a quiet, disconcerting drive from her small bungalow to The Moon Glow. Nicki remained pensive, distant, almost desperate. Not what Mike was hoping for, even if his feelings for the beautiful girl were still vague. He had imagined himself as a knight in tarnished armor, whisking away the troubles of the day.

Nicki picked at her dinner, preferring to sit quietly and stare at her plate. She seemed to struggle with herself and eventually she lost. She ordered a double Scotch, and Mike watched as the girl tossed the drink back like a sailor. He said nothing. The alcohol seemed to relax her a little and a meaningless conversation began. Mike feigned interest in the comings and goings of sea turtles, trying to lure Nicki into a discussion about herself, but she side-stepped him.

"Why don't we get out of here?" he said. "I'm sure we could find better things to do elsewhere."

"What could we do?"

Mike leaned across the table. "There's this great little place called The Stumble Inn. Drinks are great and you can get a snack there that suits you better."

Nicki looked embarrassed. "I'm sorry about dinner," she whispered. "I guess I'm just not hungry."

"Well, they've got a little dance floor there and a pool table. What do you say?"

Nicki smiled for the first time that evening. "Okay," was all she said.

The neon flickered above the Stumble Inn. Few cars dotted the lot. Mike wondered if Big Ed and his large-breasted sea-goddess were holding court tonight. It didn't matter. What he really wanted to know was if the same cretins were sitting in the same chairs, scared shitless about what crept around outside. It would be hilarious if they were. It would be even better if they were still wearing the same clothes.

Once inside, he got his answer. It was a definite 'maybe'. Most of the clientele looked familiar. Big Ed was not in attendance, neither was his girl. The pool-shark waitress was cruising the floor in search of empties and the music was lower, but still plenty loud.

"Ever been here before?" Mike asked Nicki.

"Can you believe it? No."

"Don't know how you could've missed this," he laughed. "Here, let's grab a seat." Mike guided her to an unoccupied table, and the two sat down.

The waitress-hustler spotted them almost immediately and sauntered over. "See you found your way back, hon."

"Can't stay away."

"Want a menu?"

Mike looked at Nicki. She shook her head.

"Nope, just a beer and a...."

"Scotch, please," Nicki added.

"That's a simple order. I'll be right back."

As the waitress retreated, Mike watched the curve of her butt switch back and forth provocatively. Was she hot, or was Mike just horny? He swallowed hard and his attention returned to the prettiest girl in the joint. Nicki's eyes looked into his.

"Want to dance?" he asked.

"If you do."

He took her hand and tugged her to her feet. It was a slow song. An old one - "I'll Never Dance Again" by Herman's Hermits. Mike liked the jukebox in this place. He pulled Nicki towards him until the curve of her breasts pressed up against his chest and his arms encircled her waist. Together they moved about the small parquet square that made up the dance floor. Mike's hands moved below her waist, feeling her firm bottom lightly. She didn't flinch. He wanted to kiss her, but her head was buried in his shoulder. He wished they were alone.

A few dances and a few drinks later, Nicki suggested a drive to Bonita Bay. The nagging concern over Sheila Barton's welfare was at the root, but the thought of walking along a moonlit beach on a beautiful evening with a stunning creature like Nicki appealed to Mike.

The Corvair rumbled into the shell covered parking lot that hugged the edge of the bay alongside Fisherman's Cove. Mike jumped out of the convertible without opening the door. He did it with a stab of childish awkwardness that brought an unexpected, but welcome, smile to Nicki's pouting lips. Mike caught her grin from the corner of his eye.

As they walked towards the shore, he felt the sand welling up around the tops of his shoes, seeping into his socks and creeping down between his toes.

"You know," he said, scrunching up his face, "if there's one thing I hate, it's sand between my toes. Worse than having dirt on my hands."

Nicki laughed.

"I mean it... I can stick my hands down in mud and gunk, that's okay, but I've got to know I can wash it off when I'm done. Sand never comes out of anything. I hate sand."

"Well, if you hate it, why did you come here?" Nicki asked.

"Hell, this is Pine level," Mike grinned. "What else is there to do?"

"Not much," she whispered, looking towards the incoming waves. They were blue black and capped with a creamy white lather that rolled up on the sand. "Not much at all," she whispered again, as if all hope had left her body.

Mike grasped Nicki's shoulder, leaning on it for support. "Let me pull my shoes off, that'll help," he said, tugging at the heel of one with his free hand. "Which way now?" he asked, letting loose of her.

"Does it matter?"

"No, I guess not."

They walked a while, and the quiet suited Mike just fine. Mike just wanted to be alone with Nicki. He wanted to hold her and kiss her, but her insistent sense of doom gave him little opportunity. He was going crazy inside. Outwardly, calm and casual, but inside frustrated as hell. As the conversation wore on, Mike looked for a way to shift into a better mood, where a display of affection would not seem embarrassing. He saw the jetty separated the bay from the cove on the other side.

"Let's climb up there," Mike suggested. "We can see the beach from those rocks."

Nicki shrugged her acceptance and headed for the prominent ridge that cut the two sections of the beach apart.

The jetty was wet and glistening in the moonlight. Seaweed hung from the more jagged edges of the rocks. Tiny crabs ran for cover as Mike and Nicki approached. The rocks were home to a lot of living things. Most of the shore was submerged as the tide swelled to cover all but a few feet.

"Give me your hand," Mike said, reaching out to help her climb the slippery surface.

She paused for a second, then placed her hand in his. "Be careful you don't cut yourself," she warned. "These rocks can slice your foot open like broken glass."

"I'll be careful," he returned. "Just you be careful."

With Mike's help, they climbed up to a flat outcropping of stone, somewhere shy of the crest. A large cluster of water-worn rocks loomed above their heads like a massive porch awning.

"Let's sit under here," Mike suggested. "It looks kind of cozy."

"Cozy?" Nicki muttered. "It's chilly."

"No, come on... sit down," he said, dropping his rump onto the damp surface.

Nicki grimaced at the thought but lowered her own shapely rear on the rock beside Mike, who had yet to release his grip on her hand.

"The beach looks great from here, don't you think?" he asked, attempting to work his fingers in between hers. "It's just like a picture in one of those vacation brochures."

"I love the ocean... it's my life," she said with a lonely sigh. "I guess it always has been, though maybe I didn't know it."

"What's the fascination?"

"I don't know... maybe it's the unknown... the mystery of it all. It's ever-changing... never quite the same. And the energy of the waves... rising, crashing... falling back, then crashing again."

"Sounds like you've been giving it a lot of thought."

"Hell, it's Pine Level," Nicki said. "What else is there?"

"I couldn't agree with you more," Mike answered, moving very close to Nicki's face. "You know, you worry me," he said, but she didn't answer. Her eyes were far away, perhaps on the water, but he suspected they were somewhere farther. She noticed his breath on her cheek and turned her face towards him. Then he kissed her. Light and testing, almost as if by accident. He waited, heart pounding, wondering at her reaction. She froze, not seeming to comprehend at first, but after a moment her features softened somewhat and her eyes responded. Mike knew then that he would not get his teeth knocked out. There was an unsure moment and then he leaned towards her and their lips met again.

Time evaporated as Mike and Nicki clung together on the towering rock. Their lips moved against each other, like it was their first time. Mike did not pull away, but let his hand travel up to her face, stroking her cheek, tracing the curve with his fingers down to her chin. She made no move to break away. Joining him, she became an anxious participant.

His fingers lingered on her chin, cradling it, guiding her movements. After a while, he moved his hand from her face, gliding it along her throat and shoulders. He pressed his fingertips against the bulge of her breast, letting it rest there. She did not resist. He massaged her lightly, wondering how far this could go. She snuggled up to him even closer, giving him the answer. He worked the buttons of her blouse until the shirt fell off her shoulders. He slid his hand inside the cotton cloth and felt her nipples harden in the cool sea breeze. He rubbed her soft flesh in a pleasing manner and squeezed her other breast. Nicki's tongue darted into his mouth. Something good was happening. Something both of them needed.

Mike pushed her blouse down to her waist and pulled away from their long kiss, lowering his head to kiss her breasts. In the moonlight, they appeared to be sculptured bronze. Browned by the sun and swollen with maturity. He pressed his open lips against one tightened nipple, letting his tongue brush against it. Nicki moaned her approval as Mike bit her lightly, holding her tiny bud hard between his teeth. He moved over to the other side after releasing her breast. Before he could lift it to place a kiss upon it, something occurred to him.

It was already wet. A droplet of blackish ooze the size of a quarter had just landed on the beautiful girl's nipple. Mike looked at it, puzzled. She had her eyes closed, thinking nothing unpleasant about the moist sensation on her nakedness. A second larger droplet splashed onto her smooth brown skin. Mike reached out and smeared the goo off her breast, but another, even larger glop of slime instantly replaced it. He looked up slowly at the rock ledge above them.

"Nicki?" Mike whispered.

"Yes," she said, half opening her eyes.

What remained of Sheila Barton dropped into her face.

Nicki screamed as Mike pulled her forward towards him.

Sheila's ravaged body dangled head down from the twisting rocks above like a grotesque puppet. The face was nothing more than a ripped away mass of raw meat with one pale, glossy eye staring out of it. Most of the flesh on her chest and abdomen was gone. The arms, likewise, stripped of their muscle. Crabs scurried out of the different gouges and cavities in the corpse, searching for a hiding place. A large starfish had already attached itself to what remained of her forehead, its long arms entangled in whatever hair remained on the skull.

Mike hurried Nicki down to the beach. Shivering in the breeze, which had suddenly become an icy blast. He pulled off his jacket, draping it over her shoulders as he hurried her toward the parking lot and the security of his car.

"Could that be who I think it is?" Mike asked her.

In her shocked condition, the girl could not answer.

"I think the doctor... Politzer might figure it out. Right now, let's just get out of here."

"It must be her... it must be," she cried, collapsing into a shivering mass in his arms.

"Come on," he urged her. "Let's get back."

Mike lifted Nicki's trembling body and placed her in the car. He revved the engine and skidded the Corvair onto the road. It was twenty minutes back to town, but he made it in ten.

It was the second killing at Pine Level in as many days. Mike wondered if all this trouble had just been waiting for him to arrive. Would it turn the sleepy town into a nervous wreck? Pieces were drifting together... or apart, depending on one's perspective.

# CHAPTER FOURTEEN

— . —

T HE BRIGHT LIGHTS INSIDE the Municipal Building eerily contrasted with the almost total absence of people. Mike waited motionless on the bench in the hallway. Nicki sat beside him, sunk deep into his ribs with her head resting on his shoulder. It seemed like they'd been there for hours. Sheriff Lynch, appearing more ragged than tired, walked out of the lab, scanning the report stuck on his clipboard. Even though he was not as slow-witted as Mike had initially suspected, Lynch was pretty overwhelmed at the moment. He walked towards Mike and handed him the report.

"This is the weirdest thing," remarked the sheriff, shaking his head.

Mike made a quick survey of the report's content. Some details could easily raise even the sturdiest eyebrow. He looked at the last few lines and Lynch was disbelieving. "That's impossible," he stated, laying the clipboard down.

"You want to take your pictures now?"

"Guess I'd better," Mike replied. He turned to Nicki. "You wait here. I'll be out soon." He gave her forehead a kiss and started walking.

Lynch followed at his heels. "You know something, kid?"

"What?"

"You got bad timing."

"No shit."

Nicki watched as both men disappeared behind the door at the end of the hall. She sat rigid for a long moment, then almost absentmindedly, she picked up the forgotten clipboard. Something caught her eye at the bottom of the report and made her afraid again. She placed the board down as if it were a hot iron and stared straight ahead.

The surgical tools made an irritating sound as Dr. Politzer dumped them onto the metal tray. He was tired as he attempted to unwrap the chrome instruments, but his enthusiasm for the moment had not diminished one bit. He looked up as Mike and the Sheriff entered the lab.

"Back again, Mr. Reardon?" he said, almost relishing his role in the whole grisly affair.

"Yeah, I thought the police only worked 24 hours a day in the movies."

"Show him the body," Lynch said.

"Absolutely," Politzer beamed. "This one's something." The doctor grabbed the edge of the bloody sheet, preparing to pull it back, but Mike reached out, interrupting his wrist.

"I've seen it already, remember?" he said. "Just show me the coup de grâce."

Politzer relaxed, a little disappointed, but undaunted.

"Certainly," he continued. "The neck's the best part, anyway. Look here..." The sheet drew back, revealing the gouged-out hole. The windpipe was laid bare, resembling a pale gray garden hose chewed by an anxious puppy. The massive carotid artery hung out of the wound like a wet strand of purple yarn.

Mike covered his mouth, fighting back the nausea that swept over him. He leaned closer, staring into the gaping hole.

"Watch out, kid," Lynch warned him. "Do you remember what happened last time?"

Mike ignored him. "This is incredible," he said, putting the camera up to his eye. He clicked off a few pictures, changed his angle, and clicked a few more.

"Satisfied, Reardon?" Politzer asked.

Mike stood up, his face pale, his mouth dry. "Yeah, I guess so. You happy, Sheriff?"

"Thrilled."

"Then observe this," Politzer said, reaching into the wet, sticky rut of raw flesh with his gleaming chrome forceps. Mike gagged as the points of the tongs pushed into the bloated meat, releasing a small, rancid trickle of blood and gore that gushed out onto the table.

"Keep your eye on this," the doctor pronounced, almost proudly.

"What are you going to do?" Mike asked. "Pull a fucking rabbit out of there?"

"Not quite, Reardon. I'm certain no rabbit could have left this behind..." Politzer's forceps grabbed onto something deep inside the throat. He wrestled with it for a few seconds, pulling it free with one hard yank.

"Voila," he exclaimed, holding the forceps up to the light. In the grasp of the shiny metal thongs was a long, ivory-colored tooth. Not human, but sharp like a knife. It was new.

"God damn! I knew it!" exclaimed Lynch. "It would turn out like this. Son of a bitch!"

Politzer eyed Lynch's anxiety with a sense of pride and achievement. Blood turned the old guy on. He waved the tooth back and forth in front of Mike's eyes as if tempting him with a piece of candy, then placed it in the tray. With renewed vigor, he dug back into the wound and within seconds produced another identical tooth.

"The body must have washed up on the jetty during the early hours at high tide," Mike speculated. "She became wedged in the rocks when the tide went out."

"Figures," concluded Lynch. "It was well up there... I doubt she walked on her own."

"Well, gentlemen," interrupted Politzer. "She may have been washed onto the jetty... or she may not have."

Lynch looked at the doctor.

"If you're going to flip out Doc, will you please do it at home? I gotta get back to bed."

"All I'm saying, Sheriff, is this woman may have been killed by a shark... or maybe only something like a shark."

"What do you mean... like a shark?" asked Mike.

"It's her lungs... what's left of them," the doctor began. "There's no water in them. None. And this..." He reached down with the forceps, scooping up a stringy mass of gooey mucous. "Saliva... in large quantities."

"Yeah... so what?"

"Fish don't salivate."

Lynch just sighed and hung his head. "Get on with it," he said.

"This woman may have been killed on land."

Mike searched his groggy brain for a response. "Could anything else do this?" he asked.

Politzer poked at the loose teeth in the tray.

"They could with a mouthful of these."

Lynch was getting grumpy. "So you're telling me that a... whatsis killed this... person on the beach?"

"Of course not. She could have been killed by someone and thrown in the water. Sharks are scavengers by nature, you know."

"What other animal is like a shark?" Mike wondered. "Barracuda?"

"That, Mr. Reardon, is the most fascinating aspect of this entire adventure," Politzer said.

"You call this an adventure?" Lynch sneered. "I'm going home. You too, kid... I expect to see you back in here by noon, got it?"

"Yeah, okay."

Late in the night, the door to the Triton Project Lab swung open. Cool, milky green light seeped through the darkness, glowing from within. A figure appeared in the rectangular patch of brilliance. It was Gail, or at least it was a tired human shell masquerading as Gail. She walked out, leaving the door ajar, and crossed the small lot to the woods that bordered it. Doubts and apprehensions swirled in her brain as she went through a routine that had long ago come to sicken her. She entered the woods, though she had no desire to, and began searching the ground with the beam of her flashlight.

Why didn't they just pack it in? she wondered. People were getting killed. The project had everything it needed. Why couldn't they just leave? 'No', she'd been told. They weren't doing anything wrong. Just stay with the program, Sylvia had insisted. Now Gail found herself in the middle of nowhere, searching for living prey like a wild jungle beast.

Up ahead, she found what she was searching for. It glimmered in the pine filtered moonlight. Her beam traveled over the surface of the wire box set by Sylvia to entrap small unwary game. The rig had done its work and Gail sensed something living inside that manufactured cage. She crept forward, kneeling down to peer into the darkened trap. Inside was a frightened house cat. The feline arched its back and spat menacingly at Gail as she stared at it with her light.

"Hello kitty," she purred. "You want to go home with me?"

She picked up the cage, making no attempt to set the animal free, and started back towards the Triton Project with the 'Catch of the Day'.

Inside the building, she placed the trap on one of the many lab tables. "Poor thing," she said to the nervous cat. "I wonder if anyone will miss you?"

Sylvia entered from another room and crossed to the cage. "What is it?" she asked.

"House cat."

"She'll do just fine," she said. "Check and see if Michelob's doing alright."

Gail nodded and crept to the other side of the lab. Nicki would kill them if she found out what they had done to her dog. The wretched little pup. She should have never left him at the lab. Funds had been running low for some time. They had little choice, but that didn't untangle the knot in Gail's stomach. She thought about the lovable little animal and what the experiments had done to him.

She lifted the drape that was covering a tank and looked into it. Under the cloth was a large glass aquarium with a series of air filters flowing through it. The murky water was just clear enough to see the thing on the bottom.

Gail bent down to see the small creature in the tank. It was a foot and a half long and looked like a mix of small terrier and catfish. Its skin was smooth and pebbled, not scaly, and it had three sets of pulsating gills on either side of its head. The head was dog-like, but the body had no limbs and resembled an eel. Above all else, the most striking thing about the monstrosity was its eyes. Large, bright eyes that spoke of a great sadness inside. Gail couldn't look into those eyes. Shame wouldn't let her.

"How are you today, boy?" she asked.

The little creature lifted his head and made a slight wag of its eel-like tail, but it didn't seem thrilled to see her. Gail pulled out a small cellophane wrapped packet from a nearby drawer and dangled it in front of the aquarium glass.

"Want a biscuit?" she cooed, unwrapping the packet. She pulled out a hard little tidbit shaped like a piece of cheese and waved it over the tank. Michelob, or what had been Michelob, looked up at the treat being offered, but made no move. She got the message and dropped the biscuit into the tank. The little mutant watched as it drifted down to the bottom, moving forward to suck in the soggy treat.

"He doesn't seem very happy," Gail said.

"He doesn't have to be happy," Sylvia snapped. "Just healthy."

Gail smiled weakly, fighting back her guilt, as she watched the creature work over the dog biscuit. "Well, at least he still enjoys his treats."

Sylvia crossed to the tank to look at the mutant herself. "He's getting a little bigger," she said. "Better cut back on his dinner, or we'll be needing a larger tank."

"Sylvia... I don't know if this is such a good idea. Any of this... maybe it's time to clear out."

"Don't be ridiculous. Nobody's clearing out," Sylvia said. "We've gone too far to talk like that. This is not work you can just walk away from."

"I can't get Stephen out of my mind."

"Don't start going manic on me, Gail. What happened to him wasn't just an accident. It was a scientific break-through."

"And Sheila...?"

"She knew the risks."

"Maybe, but I don't think she would have approved of the result... if she were still around, that is."

Sylvia turned towards Gail, giving her a stare that could have frozen lava. "Are you thinking of ducking out on me, Gail? Is that what's on your mind?"

"You know damn well that's not what I meant," she protested.

Sylvia stepped up to Gail, pushing her long fingers into the girl's hair. She tightened her grip until her knuckles whitened and gave Gail's head a strong twist to one side. "Never think of leaving me," she said with a sly smile. "I love you too much."

When Sylvia ran her tongue over Gail's lips, her junior assistant's knees almost buckled. "Let's lie down for a while," Sylvia purred. "You'll feel better. You know you will." She tugged Gail's hand, and after a moment's resistance, Gail followed her out of the room. She wondered which one of them would get to 'feel better' this time.

# Chapter Fifteen

— · —

ABOUT 1:30 A.M., THE Jenny Lynn cruised into the Gulf-side marina just south of Pine Level. It was an old tug of a charter fishing boat that ran at night. The signal lights were glowing and the ancient vessel resembled a floating Christmas tree as it did its slow turn in for the dock. A few, weary passengers hung on the rails, eager to tie-up and depart.

Skipper, Ron Cananga, came forward, leaving the piloting to his girlfriend, Jill. He looked over at the droopy-eyed fishermen and shook his head. Everyone was disappointed. Word of a killer shark had spread quickly, and everybody wanted to go home with a piece of him. Almost a dozen people had gone out with dreams of hooking the beast and displaying its dead carcass in the local paper. Luck, however, was not running high that evening. They landed a few kingfish, but nothing of interest happened. It was just another night on the Jenny Lynn.

Jill drew the boat up to the dock, and Ron threw a rope onto the aged wooden planks. He jumped onto the platform and grabbed the line, tying the boat down. He trotted to the rear of the craft and pulled the mooring rope from its clasp. In seconds, he had that end of the boat secured as well.

He lowered the ladder from the side of the cruiser. "That's it for this evening. Better luck next time."

"Ain't gonna be no next time," grumbled one discontented angler.

Ron ignored him and kept the idle banter going. "Don't forget your fish," he reminded them. "Name tags are on them."

Jill came out of the steering cabin, lending a hand to the older people who had chanced a night on the boat. She was pretty and sexy in an earthy way. Jill had a little meat on her bones but was not fat. She sported a great tan, culled from months of fishing excursions in the gulf, and a curly head of coffee-colored hair. Her hips were full, but the waist was tiny and flowed upward into a terrific bosom. She made a pleasant contrast to Cananga, who was smallish, but muscled, with deep, weathered lines carved into his features. His arms were striated with cable-like tendons, developed from years of pulling line and operating the boat alone. His was a hard life, but not without reward. He now owned the boat he had once worked on as a mate and he had Jill. That made everything worthwhile.

Now the night's run was over and the last passengers were gathering their belongings and disappearing down the dock.

"How'd we do?" Jill asked.

"Not bad... not good, but not bad," he said. "Better for this time of year, but then a little shark scare brings out the Great White hunter in all of them," he kidded. "Let's grab a beer."

"You go ahead. I'm hitting the shower."

"Can I watch?" Ron smiled.

"I'll leave the door unlatched," she laughed.

He admired her form as she sauntered towards the lower cabin where their living quarters were. What a woman, he thought as he watched her butt swing back and forth with that taunting little walk she did.

Jill was a real find and a great worker, too. In just a few months, she had learned the tricks of operating the boat, and never uttered a whimper of complaint. Great lover too, Ron mused. She knew every way imaginable to draw him out of a foul mood. She could drive a man crazy. He was counting on it.

Ron hurried forward to the captain's cabin, where he kept the beer on ice. He climbed up the steps to the darkened booth and felt around for the cooler. Down below, he heard the shower come on.

He reached into the icy slush and grabbed a can. It was a welcome relief after pandering to a boatload of whining tourists all evening. It wasn't much fun, but it was a living, and it helped pay for the boat. Ron was lucky, he figured. A lot of guys had given up on Pine Level and moved their business up the coast. He was just too stubborn in his ways to be run off by a little poor luck, and besides, with most of the other skippers gone, the competition dropped off altogether.

He popped the tab on the brew and took a long draw. It burned his throat with marvelous freezing fingers as it went down. The sound of the shower pattering below reminded him that there was a naked girl down in the cabin slick with a soapy lather. He pulled off his shirt and wiped the salt from his brow with it. He was imagining how good a shower would feel after a long, dull night. Unbuckling his canvas belt, he found out.

He hopped down the varnished wood steps that led into the lower quarters and followed the sound of running water. The cabin was dark with a splash of amber thrown upon it by the two lanterns in the room. The place resembled the captain's quarters of old, with aged nautical maps and seafaring trinkets collected through the years adorning the walls. Yellow illumination emanated from the crack under the door, streaking the steam that snaked out with an eerie light. He kicked off his deck shoes, dropped his pants over the back of the chair and rapped on the door.

"Ron?" came a call from within.

"No, Ron's gone off. I've just come to read the meter, Miss. Do you mind?"

"Why yes," she played along. "As long as you're not the mailman, I guess it's okay."

Ron pushed the door open and stepped into the foggy depths of the craft's tiny bathroom.

Outlined in the swirling mist, he could make out Jill's shape. It was not too tall, deep bronze, possessed two large breasts and a tiny curly patch shaved on the sides. It was hard to see through the steam, but he was looking.

"Mr. Meter Man," the shape gasped in a little girl's hushed voice. "You're not wearing any clothes!"

Ron looked down at his achingly aware body and grinned. "I didn't want to get my uniform wet. Is that a problem?"

"Not at all, but please hurry and read my meter. I've got shopping to do."

"Aye, aye, first mate Jill."

"Screw the aye, aye, shit," she said. "Let's just mate!"

Ron stepped into the hot spray and placed his arms around her waist. He kissed her, long and hard, letting his fingers run down the small of her back to her well-shaped cheeks. He cupped her muscled buttocks and squeezed them as her tongue drove its way into his mouth. Her hardened, soapy nipples flattened themselves against his chest. Ron thought that this kind of moment made each day worthwhile. Her slippery body glided against his, her pelvic area grinding against his hardness as he slid his hand deep between her cheeks and felt a new, sensual wetness.

"Do me here," she whispered huskily, raising one leg to allow his fingers to probe deeper into her. "Right here in the shower."

"All right, honey," he said, biting her shoulder.

Jill's hand reached down, grasping him, guiding him into her. He lifted her, sliding deep within. Her moan was soft but audible in his ear. "Oh God," she whispered in a tone Ron knew well. It meant he had touched just that spot that Jill loved most. It was the touch that caused her to shiver under the rush of the hot water. He pulled back a little and thrust harder, deeper. Her fingernails dug into the back of his neck. Her small sounds grew louder. He knew that soon his own would join her sounds. Her breath came hard.

Suddenly, the boat rocked violently to one side. It threw both lovers off balance, sliding to the floor, entwined.

"Goddamnit!" Ron exclaimed. "What the hell was that?"

"Maybe one passenger forgot something," Jill gasped.

"If that's what it is, they must weigh a ton."

"What are you going to do?" she asked.

"Hell, I'm going up to check it out," he said, running his hands over her soapy breasts, pinching the nipples. "Stay calm," he said. "I'll be back in a flash."

He stepped out of the shower and grabbed his trousers. She watched anxiously as he climbed out of view.

On the upper deck, he grabbed his pistol from its hiding place near the cabin door. He checked the cylinder, making sure it was loaded, and started for the steering booth.

The breeze had turned into a light wind, causing the rigging to rattle eerily, but he could find no trace of anyone. The lights dotting the marina flickered in the battering wind, but the dock itself seemed deserted. A sound, rough and grating, crept to his ears. It came from the back and clattered like a metal bucket being struck with a tire iron.

"Okay, who's back there?" he called.

No answer.

Ron waited a moment, then cocked the gun. He crept back toward the sound, edging around the side of the steering booth.

Near the bait trough, he could see a dark shape. Something big, digging around in the containers, grabbing, scratching.

"Okay, pal," he said. "Hands up."

The shape stopped rummaging and turned towards him. It rose to its full height and looked down on the annoying little man. Ron could see the intruder now. It was immense. Nightmarish. Black, shiny, still dripping wet with ocean water. In its massive, razor-lined jaws it clutched the bits and pieces of live bait that were its dinner.

Ron stared, but couldn't find the correct instinct to get his feet moving in the right direction. The creature seemed reluctant to move as well. A low growl reverberated in its throat. Ron dug deep, finding the strength to squeeze the trigger of the .38. The gun ripped a hole in the thing's chest when it blasted a loud report.

The monster howled in pain as the bullet lodged in its thick hide. It reached up and poked a finger into the dime-sized hole. Blackish blood spurted forth, confusing the monstrosity. This never happened before and it hurt.

Cananga snapped out of his trance and began firing at the intruder. Hole after gaping hole opened up in its hide until the thing lunged toward him, batting the pistol aside. The creature howled in pain and anger as it reached for Ron's head, clamping large, clawed hands on either side of his face. The thing gritted its rippling teeth as it applied increasing pressure to the man's skull. Ron let out one long, bone chilling scream before his head caved in, exploding in a gory shower of blood and brains.

The creature hurled the limp corpse over the side and began nursing its wounds. It looked at the six holes dotting its chest, smearing the seeping blood with its claw.

Jill was turning off the shower, wondering what had become of her lover. The water rushing over her head had drowned out any noises that might have drifted down from the deck above. She stepped naked out of the bath and crossed to the bed, wrapping a towel around her wet hair.

"Ron," she called up top. "Come on honey, I'm still horny. Get your sweet ass down here and finish me."

Above her, she heard the heavy thud of footfalls on the upper deck. She pulled out a bottle of body lotion and spread it over her breasts and down between her legs. "Baby, hurry. I am so hot for you!" she squealed in a poor imitation of a sex-starved French love maid. "Please, geeve eet to meee," she pleaded.

No answer came, only the thud of footfalls and the soft splash of water against the side of the boat. The steps appeared to circle above her head. They seemed to be near the steps that came down into the cabin.

"I'm in heat, baby, and I'm going to fuck the brains out of the first man who comes through that door!" she teased, letting her fingers linger between her open thighs.

Suddenly, the cabin door leapt off its hinges and heaved over the side. Jill screamed as the lumbering black shape pushed its colossal form into the cabin, squeezing through the small portal. It looked around once in confusion before spotting her.

She scampered across the bed, hurling a pillow into the face of the thing. It swatted at the object, slicing it open and sending thousands of tiny feathers into the air. The fluff swirled about the monster's head, bewildering it. Feathers stuck to its slime coated face and clogged its gills, causing it to choke and gasp for air.

Jill was terrified, but she saw the opportunity to escape. As the creature clawed in agony at the dampened feathers lodged in its gills, she made a mad dash past it, crawling up the steps. The beast dug its sharp nails into the soft tissue beneath its gills, trying to scrape out the wet feathers that were becoming soaked in the beast's own blood. The pain was unbearable. It kept clawing and digging. It was on the verge of suffocating.

Jill ran naked down the dock, trying to reach the parking lot. As she passed one of the other boats, she seized a canvas sailor's bag to wrap around herself. Behind her, she heard the monster's frenzied roar of despair as it climbed out of the cabin in a strangling panic. In one huge lunge, it threw itself overboard and disappeared. The marina fell silent behind the running girl.

The creature swam out, away from the boats, gulping in the cold ocean water, forcing it to pass through its mouth and back out over the damaged, bloody gills. It felt better now. Soon it would be back to normal. The saltwater sent burning tendrils of pain into the bullet holes that riddled its chest, but those too would heal in time. The salt was good for them, but it burned. Humans were a pain in the ass.

Maybe it would have to get rid of them. All of them.

# CHAPTER SIXTEEN

—·—

N ICKI'S BUNGALOW WAS DARK when Mike's Corvair pulled into the driveway. After shutting off the engine, both of them sat in the gloom. Finally, he pushed the door open and got out. He circled the car and helped Nicki stand up. Together, they walked towards the bungalow.

Inside, the harsh light of a bare overhead bulb blasted away the dismal murkiness. Nicki crossed the room, switching on a softer lamp.

"You can turn that off now," she said, showing the ceiling light. Mike flipped the switch and walked over to the small couch, literally collapsing on it. Nicki joined him, laying close on the edge. His arm circled her shoulders and held her close.

She stared straight ahead, tired eyes focused on an invisible spot on the wall across the room. "Don't leave me tonight," she whispered. "Please don't leave me alone."

"Don't worry. Big Ed himself couldn't throw me out."

He put his cheek next to hers, kissing her ear.

She lay still for a few minutes, staring ahead, feeling Mike's hand resting against her breast. Her head turned as she looked at him.

"Mike?" she whispered.

"Yeah?"

"Can I talk to you about something?"

"Let it wait until morning, honey? You need to sleep."

"I can't sleep."

"Okay," Mike said. "Talk to me."

"Triton..."

"Triton? Are you sure you aren't just over-tired and don't know it? I'm beat and I got the word straight from up top to be in early tomorrow."

"Look Mike, I don't know if the lab has anything to do with this, but if it does, I can't hold back any longer. Every time you look at me, I feel guilty. I'm nervous you're going to find out something terrible and hate me for hiding it. I can't sleep or even think with it on my mind."

"Okay, I'm sorry," he said. "I knew something was bothering you, but I didn't want to push it. If you're ready to talk about it, I'm ready to listen."

"It'll sound crazy to you, but it's the God's truth. It began with our work on the sped-up growth of sea ferns. The research was all-consuming. It took up every minute of our days."

Mike tried hard to suppress the yawn that forced its way towards his lips.

"It was exciting. I mean, it was the breakthrough we had been waiting for. Sylvia had a special enzyme we distilled from one plant that altered the genetic structure of whatever ingested it. The formula came from a special project based in Washington. We started a bed off the rocks at the edge of the bay, despite the sea ferns being Indonesian. The plants supplied us with everything we needed and we took it from there."

"Whoa, you're losing me in the kelp beds, kid."

"What I'm trying to say is that these pure enzymes could change the tissue structure of the host organism and if broken down into its basic elements, it could recombine with another living genetic structure creating a unique, hybrid life form."

Mike sat up, rubbing his eyes. The information sounded like so much scientific gobbledy-gook, but the way Nicki talked, it convinced him she believed it. Grasping the real meaning behind it, however, was something else. "I don't understand a thing you've told me," Mike admitted flatly.

"We could combine the plant enzyme with the DNA of a living organism, inject it into a snake, and the snake would take on the attributes of an aquatic animal."

"That is very comic book," he said wearily.

"But true. I swear it. Sylvia refused to communicate any of our findings to the foundation and they pulled our grant. She has a tight contract on the facility itself, but I couldn't afford to hang on any longer. And there's that other thing..."

"What other thing?"

"I'm not ready to talk about it just yet. But someday... maybe."

Mike sighed. "Is this what's been eating you?" Mike prodded.

Nicki shivered in the gloom of the small bungalow, then bowed her head. "No," she continued. "There were ... experiments."

"What experiments?"

"We tried the formula out on lab animals. We created specimens that could live both in the water and on land for short periods of time."

"You mean like a frog or newt or something?"

"I know it's hard to swallow, but I was there, Mike. I know."

"Maybe that's why your friend split. Maybe he just couldn't hang on any longer either and went broke too, or maybe his mother really fell ill."

"Stephen? Not likely. He was so involved in the entire project, he refused to give up on it. He was obsessed with its success and wanted it just as badly as Sylvia and Gail. Maybe worse. He wouldn't just walk away. If his mother was sick, he'd have returned, but to just simply vanish..."

"And the lab animals?"

"Two died," she said, remembering. "Stephen killed the last one after it got loose and bit him. He got very sick but refused medical attention. Sylvia said she could treat the wound. He wasn't worried about it and didn't want to take any time off the project."

"Was that the last you saw of him?"

"He never even said goodbye."

"Maybe he was sicker than you thought and hoofed it back home to New York, like the girls said."

"Somehow I just don't buy it. He was so dedicated, so...," she left her words hanging.

He looked at her expression, trying to find a clue to the mystery that lived in the girl's head, but nothing came easy. It was like trying to pick a lock with a welding glove on.

Momentarily spent from her desire to spill her guts, Nicki laid her head back and nodded off. Mike watched her slip under and was thankful.

C OLONEL JACKSON WAS UP for hours before his alarm went off. Special orders had arrived around midnight and, even though he was determined not to open the packet until morning, sleep was rough and tenuous. He now sat at the breakfast table watching the sun rise over the backyard fence. A cup of steaming coffee sat next to the unopened packet from HQ.

He went into the darkened bedroom and switched off the alarm. Meg was still asleep. God bless those ear plugs, he thought. Without them, he wouldn't have stayed married. He picked up his eyeglasses from the night table and went to the kitchen.

He opened the packet, cutting it with a steak knife. It was one of those steak knives that never needed sharpening. Damnedest thing. Just another of life's little conveniences that Meg had introduced him to. She was a wonderful person. She kept a spotlessly clean house, cooked a well-balanced meal and dressed pretty. He was glad they'd found each other.

Years on the bomb squad had turned his hair gray, but Meg liked it that way. She even liked the creases around his eyes and tolerated his pipe-smoke. That's what women were for, he guessed. They love your poor traits and tolerate your good ones.

He pulled the dossier from the packet.

The papers inside were very similar to the ones he'd seen before. This and that, but it all came up the same - somewhere somebody was working outside their charter.

Years of combat training and his exposure to the horror in Nam had made Colonel Jackson uniquely suited to command the creature investigation unit. It was not something he had ever wanted, but after the military had detained him during the long months it took to study thoroughly, the dead creature he had found by the river that day - the thing with a missile lodged in its heart - he seemed to know and understand these beasts. He had watched for months as the doctors analyzed the thing's blood. Had even drunk a toast with the boys in white to celebrate the breaking of the genetic code. The Viet Cong had created the beast in a hidden lab somewhere, but purely by accident and like others since, had found their creation extremely difficult to control. It's a good thing they never learned to mass produce the killers. Jackson had always been thankful for that.

He was the best man for the job. He had a sense of duty and not a scientific bone in his body, therefore eliminating the chance that he would ever waver in his duty and make the wrong decision.

It was dangerous work, but he never had to face it alone. After the first few instances, they learned what force was necessary to bring the situation under control, but there were the nightmares - the nagging realization that these creatures were beyond rationalizing. No one knew how they thought or could predict what they might do. One thing was certain: it took firepower and guts to contain them. Jackson possessed both qualities.

Soon Meg would awaken, and she would ask when he was leaving. She could always read his face. He would tell her when, but never where. She had the wisdom to not ask.

Jackson wondered if she even suspected what his assignments comprised, but if she did, she never let on. She just
loved and cared for him, and that was enough.

He hated his job. He knew, subconsciously, that it scared
him, but it was important and it saved lives and that was all
the justification needed.

Jackson went back into the bedroom, kissed his sleeping
wife and packed his kitbag.

# CHAPTER SEVENTEEN

—•—

THE JANGLING OF THE telephone brought Mike bolt up-right. The sun was streaming into Nicki's living room, smarting his eyes. He turned over, trying to ignore the phone. After all, it wasn't his house. It kept ringing until he answered it. He sat up, aware the girl was no longer in the bungalow. He staggered to the irritating device and lifted the receiver.

"Hello," he muttered, still half asleep.

"Something told me I'd find you there," Sheriff Lynch said. "Been there all night, I reckon."

"Yeah," Mike said. "What time is it?"

"Quarter past one. You coming in?"

"Sure. Anything shaking?"

"Got a girl in here... run in buck naked. Says some kind of monster attacked her. Can't locate her boyfriend. She's plenty shook up."

"Where did this happen?" Mike asked, paying very close attention.

"Where the hell do you think it happened? Near the bay. Down at the marina. Couple of people said they heard some shooting, but the girl swears she fought it off with a goddamn pillow!"

"Maybe I'll skip coming in and go straight there. I can get some pictures. What's the name?"

"Boat is called the Jenny Lynn, but you won't have any trouble finding it. I sent that idiot deputy, Brooks, to rope it off."

"Okay, I'll get a shower and shoot over there."

"Fair enough," Lynch agreed. "And if you see Brooks, tell him not to hang himself with that rope."

"Gotcha," Mike said, hanging up the phone. On the small table next to him was a 5x7 color photograph in a simple metal frame. Mike picked it up for a closer look. The picture showed Nicki and a young man with thick eyeglasses. They were both wearing floppy hats and holding fishing rods and standing on a pier. Nicki looked happy and silly. The guy looked uncomfortable. Mike guessed the picture was a year old. The color was faded a little. Cheap processing, he suspected. In ball-point pen at the bottom, scrawled "Nicki and Stephen - Pelican's Nest". So this was Stephen. Not a bad-looking guy, Mike thought. A clean-cut studious type. The eyeglasses gave him a nerdy sort of appearance, but his build was sporting. Mike wondered if they'd been more than friends but guessed otherwise since Nicki didn't seem to have been in touch with him prior to his departure. He crossed the room and looked out the front window. His car was still there, but Nicki had disappeared.

He lumbered into her bathroom, switching on the light. It was a pleasant enough place, decorated with shells and other nautical stuff. The shower was the old variety with the cloudy semi-transparent plastic curtain ala PSYCHO, which was comforting. It, too, had seashells printed on it. Mike stepped inside and let the hot water rip. At first it was cold, but soon it warmed up into a scalding blast that would've boiled a lobster.

Mike finished up and dragged on his jeans. He searched through Nicki's closet, trying to find a clean shirt that would fit him, but it was sparse. There was a stack of books above the clothes. Some were volumes dealing in biology and sported fancy Latin-sounding titles, others were religious in content, though the standard Bible, per se, was not among them.

He lifted the books for a better look after seeing something white at the bottom of the stack. What he saw astounded him. They were the Polaroids of Nicki. Nude. She seemed to be asleep or unconscious in the pictures, but someone nearby in the stills had been very busy. There was a red ball gag jammed in her mouth, the strap tied around her head and tiny jaw-like devices clamped on her nipples with a short length of chain between them, holding her breasts taut and erect. Her hands were bound with rope above her head and they tied her legs spread-eagle to the bed frame, exposing her sex for the voyeuristic photographer. The next photo, even more hideous, showed an outstretched female hand reaching into the picture - the hand of the photographer. Her fingertips touched Nicki, but the young girl still lay there expressionless. Had they had drugged her, Mike wondered. That must be it. And who was the other woman in the picture? This was the dark, terrifying secret Nicki lived in fear of, and Mike knew that one of the ice bitches at the lab was behind it. He figured the sadist to be Sylvia Trent, since Gail resembled a follower more than a leader, and this was just the insurance Sylvia would demand in order to keep Nicki silent. Mike bet there was another set of these floating around, but for now, he would just replace them and say nothing.

It's just what happens when you don't mind your own business, he realized. He felt terrible for Nicki but knew it was impossible to console her. It would come out if she trusted him enough.

He settled on putting his old shirt back on and hoping no one would notice. It didn't smell too awful and besides, he was a cop. He wasn't required to smell good.

Mike coaxed the Corvair onto the road and sped off for the marina. He hadn't asked where it was, but Lynch led him to believe there was only one, and Mike remembered passing such a place driving into Pine Level. He tried to push the images of Nicki's sexual torture and abuse from his mind, but the pictures burned themselves into his brain. Did he love her? Could he love her now? Either way, he would make certain that Sylvia Trent paid for this degrading violation.

Nothing seemed amiss at the dock when Mike first pulled up. Brooks' squad car sat off to one side, red lights blazing, otherwise, things seemed pretty calm. Down at the end of the pier, Mike could see the yellow rope that surrounded the hull of the Jenny Lynn. He hurried down the dock, his fingers loading a fresh roll of film into his camera. There didn't seem to be anything out of order on the old boat. Deputy Brooks was nowhere to be seen as Mike ignored the police line and climbed aboard.

The decks were fairly clean and pretty much in order near the steering booth. At the back, near the bait troughs, he noticed several pools of blackish ichor staining the varnished wood. He took a picture of the wet stuff while he knelt. It was like the goo that had dripped onto Nicki's breast intermingled with blood.

Small puddles of wetness surrounded the trough and pieces of shredded bait lay strewn about the deck. Mike couldn't help but think about the mess he found in the bait shack. He snapped off a few more shots, noting the smattering of tiny feathers soaked into several of the slime pools.

He backed away from the foul-smelling troughs and tried his luck below deck. The hatch was wide open, so he hopped down the steps.

Inside were more pools of blackish crud and a million tiny feathers. The pillow was slashed open, and the place was a mess. Mike recorded the ugly spectacle on film before climbing topside. As he came out of the cabin, he saw Brooks walking down the dock towards him.

"How long you been down there?" the deputy asked.

"Long enough," Mike replied. "Where were you?"

"Calling Bob on the pay phone. Damn car radio is on the fritz again."

"What happened here?"

"Hell if I know," Brooks grumbled, scratching his stressed jaw. "There was some shit on the deck here earlier," he pointed. "Brains and gunk maybe, but the gulls kept diving at it and got it all, whatever it was."

"Brains?" Mike asked. "Have you ever seen brains before?"

"Well, no, but that's what it looked like to me."

"Make sure you put that in your report, Deputy," Mike muttered as he walked away. "Brains snatched by seagulls."

Deputy Brooks watched Mike stroll down the dock toward his old wreck of a car. Wise-assed city kid, he thought. Just the punk kid nobody in Pine Level had a use for. Brooks leaned over to spit in the water and something wet and shiny caught his eye. It was a clump of icky material clinging to the rail. He looked closer and knew what it was. It was a wet, wrinkled, ripped out chunk of Ron Cananga's brain tissue. Brooks' mouth stretched wide into a gargoyle's grin. He turned to call after the slick kid from Miami, but as the words departed his lips, a huge gull swooped down and plucked the tasty morsel away.

Mike retraced his initial journey into Pine Level, searching for the old bait house with the big hole in its backside. He remembered the little shack had only been a few miles from the first deserted house he had seen. A file clerk had informed him that the frightened old man who ran the place was Lankford. "Lanky" for short. His first name escaped everyone. Apparently, he only had initials where other people had names. After fifteen minutes of driving, Mike saw the ramshackle bait station huddled off the pavement a hundred yards ahead.

As before, the place seemed abandoned. He came to a stop, looking around the dump. Nothing stirred. He leaned hard on the horn, but still got no response. He turned off the radio and got out.

"Hey Pops," he called. "Customer!"

Nothing.

Apprehension welled up in a hot knot in Mike's stomach. It was too damned quiet. He didn't like it after what had gone on around Pine Level, and he was wary of opening the door. Shielding his eyes from the sun, he looked through the dark, rusty screen.

"Hey, Daddy-O," he joked. "Come on out, I want to talk to you." No answer.

Mike gave the aged door a tug, and it swung open on stiff hinges, creaking. It was so dark inside he could barely see. It would take time before his eyes adjusted, but he was aware of the buzzing noise of a hundred flies. Maybe no one had ever cleaned the dead bait from the floor.

Mike groped for the overhead light, relieved to discover the old man had replaced the bulb. His fingers found the chain and pulled it down hard. A low-intensity light hummed across the room.

Over in one corner sat the live bait tanks, but they had long since become silent tubs of stagnant, scum-coated water that smelled of dead fish and shrimp. The odor crinkled his nose as he searched the shadowy room for some sign of old Lankford.

Someone had crudely mended the hole in the back of the shack since his last visit. Patched it with a mix of tar paper and old boards, but it looked to Mike as if something had busted through again. The repair work lay ripped apart and scattered about the floor.

The sickening smell and the constant swarming of a million flies convinced him to exit from the building through the torn hole in the back wall. He looked through the gash towards the woods that lay behind the place. Everything seemed fine out there and the air was fresh and inviting. He eyed the hole in the wall and guessed it was big enough for at least two men to fit through. As before, the more jagged, wicked splinters of wood displayed a blackish sludge that was becoming all too familiar.

He placed his right foot on the edge of the gaping hole and took a light jump outward into the grassy yard behind the shack. As he leapt, his pant-leg snagged on a protruding nail head and tripped him, causing Mike to do a minor tumbling act before landing unharmed in the high weed-choked foliage that made up the rear of the bait house.

With a slight rustling sound, he rolled to a stop in the burgeoning tangle. Nothing broken or sprained, he came up into a sitting position, rubbing his head. What harm could a small fall in the grass have done? Nothing much for Mike, and nothing much for old man Lankford either, who lay stone cold dead, about three feet away.

Lankford hadn't been smart enough to pull out after he'd first seen the thing that tore an enormous hole in his place. He had tried to defend himself, Mike determined, from the old, twisted shotgun that lay like a child's puzzle nearby, but it did little good. Lankford should have high-tailed it out of there. Either way, this is how he ended up. Dumped in the high grass, flies burrowing their maggot-spawning eggs in the raw, open flesh that still resembled a man. Mike had hit his breaking point. Now it was time to throw up. Again and again. And he felt better, too.

He staggered, choking, through the grass to his car and got out his camera. Duty called. No, he thought, duty insisted. His hands shook hard, keeping him from plunging back out behind the building. He decided first to call this in from the pay phone that sat on an isolated corner of the deserted station lot.

This latest addition to the body count did not thrill Sheriff Lynch, but that didn't seem to matter much anymore. It would change nothing. Mike figured it was time to record the scene. Get in and get the hell out. That was his motto. Or at least it would be from here on.

Things around the back didn't look any different from where he stood than they had a few minutes earlier. The breeze had picked up a little, the high grass swaying. There remained a half-hidden lump of death making its own little bed in the greenery.

Mike edged forward. He almost expected the old man's body to jump up and come running towards him. That's what happened in all the zombie movies, but this was real. Slowly he crept to where he could get a clear picture of the grisly sight, his finger searching for the exposure ring. Normally he would have held his breath to take this shot, but aside from the constant upheaval in his stomach, photographing mutilated corpses was becoming passe.

He snapped off a few and wondered how long it would take before some hayseed in town got the notion Mike caused their troubles. Yeah, Mike figured, a new kid comes to town, a rash of murders ensue. Let's string that boy up. Big Ed could help knot the rope. He tried to get back to taking his pictures. The next photo might be a brilliant cover for 'Mangler's Monthly' magazine, except he never snapped it. His finger was just about the depress the shutter when a loud crack sounded.

Something small whistled past his ear, taking a chunk out of a tree ten feet behind him. Mike looked up. Someone had taken a shot at him.

He dove into the tall grass, landing next to the old man's corpse. Another shot blasted past him, finding a home on the ground somewhere off to his right.

Mike crawled away from the body, leaving his camera behind. He figured to snake it out on his belly until he could reach the trees bordering the bay and swim for it if he had to. Another shot whizzed past him, thudding into the old man's rotting corpse, making Lankford jump one last time. Mike kept crawling.

Fucking great, he thought. Here I am, a goddamned police officer, crawling around like a salamander on his belly without a firearm while some asshole takes pot-shots at me. He wondered if this maniac could be the killer of old Lankford. There must be a connection or else Mike wouldn't be scooting around on his stomach. He cursed himself as he crawled. Never again would he go anywhere without his gun.

The next shot fired hit far behind him, smashing his abandoned camera. After that, everything went quiet. The shooting stopped and Mike froze in mid-crawl, listening. In the distance, he heard the approaching squad car. It must be Brooks, he thought. Who else would come in, lights and sirens blazing? Thank God for that knuckle-head. He might have just saved Mike's life.

The squad car whipped into the run-down service station and Deputy Brooks jumped out. Brooks enjoyed the action that came with the killings. It was something he could brag about at his favorite watering hole after work. Every officer at Pine Level had a favorite. Brooks favored the Stumble Inn. He even inhabited Nate's Place occasionally. He patronized any joint that offered a free round of drinks to a man in uniform. Brooks delighted in describing the gruesome details to his pals, who sat awestruck, buying round after round. Nothing delighted Brooks more than to be first on the scene.

The gangly officer with the prominent jaw and jutting ears pulled out his service revolver and ran toward the back of the building. Mike climbed to his feet, shaken.

"Freeze, mister!" Brooks shouted, pointing his pistol at Mike's back.

"Easy, law-man," Mike called. "It's me."

Brooks recognized Mike the instant he turned around. He lowered his gun, feeling stupid and irritated. "I thought I heard gunshots as I drove up," the Deputy offered as a kind of explanation and apology.

"You heard right," Mike said, walking up. "Did you see anybody as you came in?"

"Nope, not a soul."

"Might've been on foot, but I doubt it. Look here."

Brooks walked over and inspected the gory, ravaged corpse.

"Sheeet damn!" he exclaimed. "That's old man Lank-ford. Guy who runs this place."

"We've met."

"Wonder who was doing all the shooting?"

"Beats me," Mike pondered. "Whoever it was stopped after they blew the shit out of my camera. Lucky for me, you came along. Thanks."

"No problem. Did it ruin your film?"

"Probably. But I might salvage some of it. Depends on how much light got in. It's probably pretty foggy, but just maybe..."

Brooks started backing away from the mangled body of the old man. "Guess I better call this in. Let the Sheriff know what's happened."

Mike cradled the remains of his 35mm camera like it was a wounded pup. "I'm going back to the station," he told the Deputy. "Gotta see if anything can be saved."

"Yeah, sure," Brooks said. "I'll take charge of things here."

Mike laid the crippled camera on the passenger seat of his car. He prodded the loose pieces with his finger. The rifle slug gleamed brightly inside the camera housing. He picked it out of the ruins and held it up for a closer look. It was barely scratched. A clue, goddamn it. Finally a clue.

# Chapter Eighteen

— · —

T HE BEACH AT FISHERMAN'S Cove was cool and deserted. Whatever footprints had remained from days gone past were now blown smooth by the wind and faded as the old cove's memory. The shell covered parking lot was empty except for a few crushed beer cans and other bits of debris. No one picked up the trash around the cove after the killings. No one went near the place.

Sheriff Lynch's car maneuvered through the dilapidated fence posts that guarded the entrance to the inlet and coasted to a stop near the west end of the lot. Lynch was in a foul mood. He'd slept little and the heat being poured on by the town officials wasn't making his job any easier. He had tried to sleep, assisted by a hefty influx of rum the night before, but an early morning call from Mayor Lou Reynolds ended any thought of that. His only consolation was the hope that he had screwed up Mike Reardon's day as well.

While Lynch had the customary sense of respect for the office of the mayor, he also despised the overgrown whale that paraded around Pine Level like an emperor. Reynolds, barely a politician, had bought his way into the job by simply owning the closest thing to resemble an industry that Pine Level had ever seen. He ran The Beachcomber Resort. It was a seasonal hangout for rich fatheads from Tampa and St. Petersburg who liked to slink down the coast for a little fishing and secretarial Hanky-panky. It had a private restaurant and bar for discreet clientele. A swanky place no one at Pine Level could afford to be caught dead in.

Overpriced, overindulgent and oversexed. Just like mayor Lou Reynolds, himself.

Today as Lynch edged out of the front seat of the squad car he had the questionable honor of escorting not only Reynolds and his slow-witted, but sweet, girl, Madlyn, on a quick survey of the much talked about massacre site. Lynch hated circuses. He hated them as a kid and he hated performing in them as an adult. One thing was for sure: there would be a lot of hoops to jump through before this clown-town investigation finished.

Reynolds heaved his bloated frame out of the patrol car and held the back door open for Madlyn. She wiggled her way from the back of the car. Her enlarged breasts expanding and falling with each breath of sea air.

"You know, Lou," she remarked. "It's only a few miles from town, but it took like forever to get here."

"Maybe it was all that cigar smoke filling up the backseat," Lynch sneered, casting an accusing glance towards Reynolds.

"Don't hassle me with trivialities, Lynch," Reynolds grunted. "These are the best cigars in Tampa."

"Yeah, I know them. My mother used to slave in those factories, rolling the stinking things when she was an orphan growing up in that rotten town," the Sheriff grumbled. "I got no use for them."

Reynolds looked around the windy cove with distaste. He had a vested interest in the well-being of the beach from a business standpoint. God help Lynch if any sand got into Reynolds shoes. The mayor was a man of purpose, and that purpose had everything to do with making cash. It didn't matter if it was by hawking over-priced drinks to stuffed shirts with their hand up their secretary's skirt or by working illegal aliens from Cuba in the sugarcane fields along State Road 28 until they dropped. Business was business. Beaches and bitches. The two never seemed very far distanced from each other.

"Let's get on with it, Sheriff," he said. "I've got a full agenda this afternoon."

"Is this where the killings happened?" Madlyn tittered excitedly.

"That's right."

"Doesn't look very dangerous to me," Reynolds huffed.

"We found the girl's body up the cove a ways. Near the rocks, further up the beach. We can walk there if you'd like."

"How far did you say it was?" the mayor asked tiredly.

"I didn't, but it's not far, Lou. You game?"

"Come on honey," Madlyn pleaded. "Let's take a walk. It'll be nice."

"Well," Reynolds groaned, "if we're going to, let's get it over with."

Lynch led the pair up the beach towards where Mike had discovered Sheila Barton's desiccated corpse. It was still a mystery how the girl had gotten so high in the rocks, but that fact, combined with Dr. Politzer's findings regarding the lack of water in the victim's lungs started Lynch wondering if the killer was, in fact, something clever. Something like a man. Crazy things were happening at Pine Level. It wasn't looking good for the tiny department and after years of handling only the most minor of routine disturbances, the police force could barely pull together to combat this terrible force.

The sketchy details were perhaps the most confusing aspect of the entire investigation. People were being found in pieces, and witnesses were talking about sea monsters. There wasn't much Lynch could make of it all, but one thing seemed certain: something came aboard the Jenny Lynn in the night, something capable of walking or crawling onto the deck of the boat and laying waste to a strong, healthy young man. Something had slaughtered Ron Cananga that night, something that was as dangerous on land as it was in the water.

Madlyn kicked up some sand up between her toes as she walked barefooted behind Reynolds. The mayor didn't notice the small shower of grit spraying against the back of his pants legs. If he had, he would've had been furious. Madlyn giggled like a child, kicking up a little more. She was star-struck in love with this blubbery behemoth who couldn't see a thing past her bra size and French-cut panties.

"That's where they found her," Lynch said, pointing towards the high rock jetty that separated Fisherman's Cove from Bonita Bay.

"Sheriff," Reynolds said. "There's no way I'm climbing up there. I just felt it was my responsibility to see the situation myself. Some folks, myself included, have wondered about the efficiency of your department and several constituents thought that perhaps a little aide from St. Pete might not be a bad idea. Just to help you boys out, you know?"

"My department is doing just fine on their own, thank you," Lynch said, but he didn't believe it. "In fact, we've closed down this beach and all like it for the next few days until this problem gets resolved. I don't know what the root of these killings is, but it's connected to the ocean. If we close the beach folks will be a damned sight safer, I reckon."

"Close the beach! Don't be an imbecile, Lynch!"

"Watch it, Reynolds," Lynch threatened, his temper rising. "Or I'll stick that cigar in your other end!"

"Sheriff," Reynolds protested. "I'm all for saving human life, especially that of the folks in our town, but this beach and the others are what little lifeblood this community has."

"Blood's the word, Mayor.. blood. Buckets of it."

"You close this beach and you'll be strangling what life we got left in this sorry-ass broken down pothole. You can't do it. I forbid it. It's just plain old common-sense Bob... why don't you try using a little? This isn't JAWS, you know."

Lynch walked over to the base of the jetty. He pointed to the jagged outcropping that formed the best foothold for climbing. "You see that?" he asked. "Those are blood stains... about three quarts' worth. Common sense tells me to find the murdering sonofabitch that caused this and put an end to him. If we don't stop this killing now, there ain't going to be any townsfolk left to enjoy all the business you seem to think this stretch of sand brings in."

"The Sheriff has a point, honey," Madlyn joined in.

"Now don't you try to push some kind of twisted form of logic on me? It won't work. These beaches are staying open and this situation is going to remain confidential. The people around here know enough to steer clear when trouble's brewing, but an official closure would make news statewide. You got that, Lynch?"

"What I'm doing is within my authority and I'm going to exercise it. As for being confidential... you might as well shine that one, Lou! There ain't no shielding what happened at the marina last night. That it happened here at Pine Level might slow it down a bit. You know how those city reporters are. Nobody cares what happens around these parts. That's the problem, always has been."

"Lucky for us, Sheriff... damn lucky," Reynolds muttered. "Now drive us back to town. I got a load of lobsters coming into the restaurant and I want to be sure I'm there to count every blessed one of'em."

"Who's gonna be around to eat them, Lou?"

"You've got an attitude problem, Bob, but you'd better snap out of it and figure on doing something quick if you want to hang on to that phony-baloney job of yours."

"I've got a shore patrol rounded up. We're going to hunt this thing in the water," Lynch said matter of fact.

"Whatever it takes, Bob, but it'd better work quick, otherwise I'm going to barbecue your ass first chance I get."

"Big talk, lobster man," Lynch laughed. "You hear that in a movie or something?"

"Just shut up and drive us back."

Lynch started up the car. "Climb in chief and we'll have you counting shell-fish in no time!" He grabbed for the backseat door and allowed Madlyn to scrunch into the rear.

"This wasn't any fun at all," she pouted.

"Come on down to the station later when you get a moment and I'll show you some real bloody photographs," Lynched offered as he threw the car in gear and screeched backwards out of the parking lot. It was a rotten day, and he wasn't in a good mood.

Things inside the Triton Project center weren't much better. Gail and Sylvia had worked into the night and fallen to sleep somewhere during the wee hours. As they slumbered, strange things were happening. Gail had passed out on a cot and was struggling in a troubled dream. Sylvia had pushed on, but eventually dosed off at the lab table where she had been compiling her notes. Michelob was feeling fine and frisky... and ready for a walk.

Without making a noise, the little mutant dog tested the screen that stretched across the top of his tank with his nose. It was strong, but he was getting stronger. His little stomach grumbled with a hunger no dog biscuit could satisfy. He knew he had to get out of his watery prison. He had seen a cat brought into the lab earlier. Perhaps it was still nearby.

The mutant pushed its muzzle up against the wire grate, but it held fast. Then it pushed harder still... the wire mesh gave a little. The mutant pushed harder and harder, each time it saw the screen bulge upward. Sensing escape, the creature dove to the bottom of the tank and looked upward towards the restraining screen that held it captive. It swam around the bottom of the aquarium three times, gaining momentum as it went, then suddenly, with as much force as it could muster the mutant dog surged upward, driving its head forcefully into the screen. It hit with such an impact that the screen burst apart slightly, painfully wedging the small creature's head in its grip.

Michelob let out a small, wet yelp as he wiggled upward, trying to force his icky, slime coated body through the rend in the wire mesh. It was painful going; the screen was cutting into the new, mutated flesh, causing a sticky black fluid to flow from his slivered veins. Hunger and an overwhelming thirst for freedom drove the little dogfish onward. It struggled for several minutes against the jagged metal until it surged outward, tearing loose of the agonizing trap.

Michelob was free.

# Chapter Nineteen

— • —

I T WAS ALMOST NOON when the sound of breaking glass first brought Sylvia to her senses. She lifted her head, not sure why she had awakened. She thought nothing of having dozed off. It was a common peril of working too hard and too late. She stretched, yawning. Gail was still unconscious on the cot in the lab's corner. Everything seemed alright.

Suddenly, another crash sounded from an adjoining room, startling her. Sylvia's eyes scanned the lab, searching for some clue to the mystery. Her eyes settled on Michelob's tank and the torn screen across the top. It ripped the mesh open in a jagged manner and bits of slimy mutant dog tissue clung to the wicked prongs. A trail of black ichor trailed down the side of the tank and made its way across the floor. The slime swerved and twisted and the creature had approached Sylvia and Gail as they slept. Whatever their former pet wanted from its sleeping masters it had thought better of it since the gooey trail then led away from the women and made a deliberate path towards the air-conditioning vent on the wall, six inches off the floor, at the back of the lab. The trail wound towards the grate where a small hole had been forced. Michelob loved to chew on things. Now he was chewing on metal grating fixtures.

"Gail," Sylvia whispered to her sleeping partner. "Gail... Michelob's out."

The girl's head rose from her pillow. "What?"

"The damned dog has escaped."

"I don't understand," Gail said as she sat up, still half asleep.

"It looks like he ate through the screen on top of his tank. Thank God he's still close by. I heard a noise in the other room."

Gail stood up and walked to the aquarium. "I wonder what's gotten into him?" she said.

"Who knows what goes through the mind of a mutation? He might have some new survival instincts that are just now changing his behavior."

"Like Stephen?" Gail wondered.

"God, let's hope not, but if true, we'll study it on our own terms this time."

"What if we can't recapture Michelob?"

"Oh, we'll catch the little sonofabitch alright," Sylvia reckoned. "He may be a mutant, but he's small and right now he's a fish out of water."

The sound of metal scraping against metal shrieked from the other room. The chilling sound sent a tingle up Gail's spine. Sylvia grabbed a net from under one cabinet and together the two women stalked in the direction the sound came from.

In the next room two things became obvious: one was that Michelob had chewed through the wires that powered the key lights, the other was that the creature had savaged the house cat they had trapped earlier.

It tore its cage open and fur and blood splattered the table. The cat's gory head dangled near the floor, held inches above the hard surface by a long sickening strand of spinal tissue. It spun like an inert Yo-Yo on the end of a meaty string, its eyes glazed wide with frozen terror.

"I think we've progressed past the Milkbone stage," Sylvia said as she ran back into the lab.

"What are you doing?" Gail asked, unable to remove her eyes from the image of the slaughtered cat.

Sylvia returned, notebook in hand. "I need to take notes on the development of the mutation."

"Are you crazy?" Gail pleaded. "We need to get out of here. That thing's dangerous!"

"It's why we have to stay. We can't let him get away. Now help me look for it."

Gail rushed to one of the storage cabinets. It held a 12-gauge shotgun and a box of shells, a holdover from the project's humble beginnings when three women lived on a lonely country road by themselves. It might have seemed a little paranoid, but Gail knew someday the gun might come in handy. She hefted the rifle to her shoulder, checked the sight, then cracked it open, inserting two shells of small game load. With a determined snap, she locked the ammo into place and pressed her finger to the trigger.

"You'd shoot your own dog?" Sylvia asked.

"Damn straight."

"Well, just try to wound him. He's not worth shit to us if you turn him into pate."

Gail threw a worried look at her co-worker and then scanned the floor. Amid the tangled fur and cat guts, she noticed a distinct trail of slippery ooze that crept behind one of the storage cabinets.

"Michelob..." she whispered. "Come here, boy... come on out."

Sylvia wasn't sure where the fish-dog had gotten off to, but she wanted him in one piece. Somewhere scurrying about the floor was the end product of years of work. Regardless of how vicious the monster might be, she was certain he couldn't survive out of the tank for long. She had created him that way. If they failed to find the creature, it would soon tire and most likely crawl off somewhere to die. If it got behind a wall where they couldn't get him, there would be nothing to do except fumigate. They had to find him while he was exposed.

Sylvia peered under one table, but the lack of a powerful light made seeing very difficult. Something might be there, she guessed, dropping to her knees for a closer look. Perhaps if she crawled under there. It was gloomy, but not unmanageable, she thought. She edged herself under the dark table. That mutant dog was somewhere nearby, and she meant to catch him. Her hand, stretched forward for support, came down in a large puddle of black slime.

"Jesus," Sylvia exclaimed as she inspected her goo covered fingers. "I think I'm getting close," she called.

Gail wasn't having any luck tracking down the little beast, but at least she was armed. She rose to her feet upon hearing Sylvia's voice and walked over to the table.

"What do you see?" she asked.

"Mutant shit I guess. You still got that 12 gauge?"

"Finger on the trigger."

"Keep it that way."

"Any sign of movement?"

Sylvia looked in the shadow under the table. "Nothing."

The shadow jumped. It moved with a terrific speed, changing, squealing, charging forward to become the sickening countenance of something that had once resembled a small, loving pet. The mutant lunged for the kill.

Sylvia screamed, rising, banging her head into the underside of the table. She struck it with such power that it split the skin of her forehead open. Blood rushed down her face in a mad surge from the cut. Michelob went wild. He threw himself on her screaming face, tearing into the blood slicked flesh with beast-like ferocity. As it ripped open the side of her cheek, Sylvia could feel Gail's hands grasping her ankles, struggling to pull her out from under the table. Inch by inch, her friend attempted to drag her to safety, but the frenzied attack seemed to last forever. Sylvia managed the wrestle the monster away from her face, but it clamped its steel jaws onto the soft flesh of her forearm.

Panic gripped her as the mutant tore at her face. She struggled to regain her some of her senses, even though the pain on her arm was tremendous. She scampered backward, dragging the monster with her, still attached below her elbow.

"Oh, my god!" Gail cried as she clawed at the small thing that hung from Sylvia's arm by its razor-sharp teeth.

"Shoot it!" Sylvia screamed. "Kill it!"

"I can't!" Gail shouted. She was too close to risk firing the shotgun.

Sylvia ran into the lab, the beast swinging from her arm. She rushed over to the chemical shelf, smashing bottles and specimen trays in her mad search for some kind of aid. Her eyes locked onto the bottle of hydrochloric acid. It was risky as hell, but she could no longer think rationally.

"Sylvia, no!" Gail screamed, but it was too late.

The woman grabbed the bottle, smashing its contents onto the creature's back. The acid produced the desired effect, eating into the beast's spine. Michelob's skin smoked and boiled under the disintegrating power of the substance. A nauseating odor clouded the room.

In an instant, Michelob released his grip and fell, howling in pain, sizzling to the floor. Sylvia's arm likewise had gotten an unhealthy dose of the corrosive fluid on it as well, and she collapsed, screaming. Gail rushed to her, grabbing a roll of cotton towelettes from the counter as she ran. She attempted to wipe and absorb as much of the acid as she could, but a lot of damage had already been done. Michelob writhed and twitched about the floor in an incredible dance of pain. The acid had eaten through most of his outer flesh, revealing a weird, twisted network of abstract bones and pulsating organs within. He lay on his side, whimpering, as his skeleton became jelly and spread out on the floor in a gathering mass of sticky putrescence. Sylvia was sobbing as Gail tended to her burned arm. The skin had blistered away under the devastating influence of the acid. Muscle was exposed, but the damage might not be permanent.

"Had to get him off, Gail..." she babbled. "The pain... had to get him off me."

"Take it easy," Gail said. "I need to take care of that arm."

"Disinfectant," Sylvia said. "Pour it on."

Gail moved Sylvia over to the daybed and went for the surviving chemicals. She found the laboratory-strength disinfectant and brought it to her.

"This is going to hurt, you know?" Gail said, opening the bottle.

"Fuck it. Pour it on... all of it."

Gail disliked hurting her friend, but she knew that there was no other way. No one could guess what types of viruses or bacteria might be introduced through the wound. She gave Sylvia a rolled towel to bite down on before pouring the blue fluid into her open, gaping wounds. She screamed as the liquid foamed and gurgled in the wet, exposed patch of flayed flesh. Gail put on the proper amount of bandage wrapping and taped the entire affair. It was better if no one looked at the wound. It would not make it heal any faster.

By the time Gail had completed her nursing duties, Sylvia had passed out. It may have been late afternoon for all she knew. Time meant little inside a lab where windows and clocks had long since lost their usefulness. The mutant was dead, and Gail was exhausted. She felt Sylvia's warm body next to hers as she sat on the edge of the cot. Gently, she raised the covers and climbed in beside her. Careful not to touch the injured arm, Gail laid her head against her friend's shoulder and dozed off to sleep.

With news of Cananga's murder swarming around the marina like gnats, it became a hotbed of activity. Sheriff Lynch was carrying out his game plan to thwart the shark, or whatever it was, by patrolling the waters off the coast. He had assembled a rag-tag crew of fishermen and all the deputies who could tolerate the ride and not get sick.

The atmosphere resembled the circuses Lynch despised, but he was the ringmaster, so it would have to do.

"Come on boys," Lynch shouted. "Get your asses on board and we'll get out of here."

The men grumbled, but they dragged themselves onto the waiting craft and settled in.

"Now we don't know what we're looking for," Lynch began. "But I figure it has to be a big hammerhead or a Mako. I don't have any idea beyond that. Whatever it is, I reckon it'll be plenty huge and make a nice trophy on the wall of the man who brings it home. The plan is to reel the thing in close to the boat... then shoot the sonofabitch. You all got your rifles?"

The men acknowledged they did.

"Good, now get the hell out there and bring me back that monster!"

As the boat engines cranked up, Lynch saw the grizzled Captain Miller walking towards him with his two sons. Each carried buckets of wet slosh meant for the boat. When Lynch looked into one bucket, his stomach took a sour twist.

"What in Jesus' name is that shit?"

"Chum, Sheriff," Miller grunted. "You know, fish heads and guts."

Lynch's entire face crinkled at the stench.

"Yes sir," Miller laughed. "That brings those sharks a'runnin'."

"Or sends them a'runnin'." Lynch countered.

Miller and his sons passed out the buckets of chum to the not too anxious deputies.

"You boys be careful now, don't nobody fall overboard," Miller said. "You going out with us, Sheriff?"

"No, I got beach duty to supervise."

"Beach duty," Miller said, scratching his beard stubble. "What the hell for?"

"Don't ask," Lynch replied. "It's just one more precaution."

# CHAPTER TWENTY

— . —

N ICKI DOVE HEADFIRST INTO the cool waters of the point that framed the edge of Lighthouse Bay. It was a quiet area, and she knew it well. She should. It bordered the Triton Project lab. After diving in, she carefully tightened the straps of her scuba gear and swam off towards the deeper part of the bay. She had little idea what she was looking for, and she realized what she was doing could be extremely dangerous. Something beyond fear kept nagging at the back of her brain, something that connected the lab to the killings. She was too knowledgeable to be picked off by a shark. Sheila was an oceanographer, she knew how to get to shore without a shark sensing any panic. Could it have taken her completely by surprise? It was possible, but Nicki thought it too odd to let it pass.

As she swam, she realized a certain, overpowering sense of loneliness that seemed to permeate the bay. She dove here countless times before, searching for small specimens to sell. The bay had always teemed with life. Now it was deserted, seemingly devoid of any living specimen except herself. The gulf was empty, but that didn't seem possible, she told herself. Something must have driven the fish away. Something they were afraid of. Perhaps the big shark theory had some validity after all.

She was about to give up when a flurry of activity caught her eye. A small school of fish was darting about thirty feet away. Maybe she was letting her imagination get away from her, as she first suspected. Why would this bay be the territory of such a fierce predator? she asked herself. She stroked over to the swarming school. The sight of them comforted her. As she drew close, she saw the reason for their frantic, darting action.

They were in a feeding frenzy... feeding on the remains of a dismembered arm. Nicki gasped, blowing all the oxygen from her mask. The hand was still clutching a fragment of cloth in its dead fingers, but beyond that it was merely a length of bone and meat, entwined in sea kelp. Nicki fought back feelings of revulsion and edged forward towards the grisly limb resting on the sandy bottom.

With icy determination, she shooed away the feeding fish and plucked the cloth scrap from between the blue fingers. It was definitely that of a female. This might be the first clue to unraveling the mystery, and no amount of churning in her stomach would let it slip away. Filled with disgust, she swam back to shore as quickly as possible. As she thrust her legs through the water, she failed to see the dark shape, almost a shadow, near the bottom. It followed her. She swam as if her air tanks were empty and her life depended on it.

Sheriff Lynch looked at the dead beach the same way he looked at the other beaches. It was, in fact, his second time around on this stretch of sand, but he kept checking, driving from cove to cove. Something was bound to turn up, he figured. Eventually, on land or in the water, it mattered little. Something had to turn up.

While the patrol was important, Lynch was bored with the routine of looking repeatedly over each empty expanse. Nothing was happening here. Nothing except... a splash.

Something had disturbed the water about thirty yards out. He concentrated on the spot, tightening his jaw as he watched for another ripple. There it was. It splashed again.

With a sudden surge of energy and anticipation, Lynch ran to the squad car nearby and pulled out the riot gun he kept in the front seat. He pumped it once and was off in the water's direction.

The swirling foam was moving closer and closer to shore. Lynch saw it coming and was ready for it. He drew the rifle to his shoulder. Maybe he could get a shot at it in the shallows. That might not be an impossibility, he thought. Most shark attacks happened in three feet of water. He knew that. Suddenly, the water broke with a tremendous rush, a figure surging upward from the waves. Lynch's finger was hard set against the trigger, his breath held tight like a professional hunter. He hesitated for only one beat, but it was long enough. Nicki rose quickly into the sights of the powerful weapon.

"Jesus H. Christ!" Lynch exclaimed. "I could have blown your head off."

"Lucky me," Nicki said morosely. She waded out of the surf, holding onto the scrap of cloth she had pulled from the dead girl's fingers. "Check this out," she said.

"What is it?" he asked, taking the shred of material from her. He wanted a better look. There was a small insignia on the scrap. A circular seal with a lot of detail and some small foreign-looking words.

"That's the Triton Project logo," Nicki offered. "I found an arm with this. I'm certain it was Sheila."

Lynch shook his head grimly. "Triton, you say?"

"That's the marine biology lab near the point. The one I used to work at."

"Yeah, I know the place. This Sheila, she worked there too, didn't she?"

"Of course," Nicki replied. "That's what I'm getting at."

"It's as clear as muddied water, Miss," Lynch said, stumped.

"The night Sheila died, she left her shirt on the beach. Mike and I found it there. It was a shirt I had given her myself. This is a scrap of a Triton Project lab shirt. Not the one she was wearing. Nothing like the one we found."

"So you're saying that someone at this lab killed your friend and dumped her body out on the jetty?"

"It seems to make sense, Sheriff, but that's not possible. "

"Why is that?"

"Only Gail and Sylvia work at the lab now and they couldn't have done this," Nicki said.

"Nobody else there?" Lynch asked. "I thought there was some college kid... what's his name?"

"Stephen."

"Yeah, that's right. What about him?"

"They said he went home... illness in the family."

This information started Lynch to thinking. He had never been dumb, but he was close to it. "Are you sure that sick person wasn't the kid himself?" he wondered.

"One of the lab animals we were working with had bitten him. It could have made him sick."

"Well, he may have quit, little lady. But I ain't so sure he's left," Lynch said accusingly. An icy trickle of sea water running down the back of his neck suddenly interrupted his train of thought. "What the...!" he blurted out, jumping from the shock.

Standing behind him, barely moving, was the creature, water running down its body, dripping onto Lynch's back.

Instinct told the lawman to retreat and empty his gun into the thing. The first blast took a sizeable chunk out of the beast's chest. Black blood spurted outward, striking Lynch in the face. He quickly pumped the next shell into the chamber, but the second blast never fired. The thing reached out with lightning quickness and grabbed the Sheriff by the shoulders, jerking him forward. Nicki watched in paralyzed horror as the monster swiftly sunk its teeth into the top of Lynch's head, taking off the entire cranial cap. A maelstrom of blood and brains flooded the surrounding beach. Lynch, not quite dying instantly from the tremendous wound, fell to the ground, his eyes twitching involuntarily as his mind ran out onto the sand.

Nicki snapped out of her trance and screamed for a lifetime's worth. The sound pierced the inner ears of the creature like knife-blades. He turned to face Nicki, his attention being drawn away from the trembling body of Sheriff Lynch that lay before it. She dropped to the ground, grappling with the gun frozen in the lawman's dying grasp. The monster watched her with a certain fascination as she struggled to free the weapon from the Lynch's death-clutch. Blood continued to gush unheeded from the wound in the creature's chest. It rained down freely, coating Nicki's arms and legs in gore. With one last yank, the gun came free and Nicki shoved the barrel into the razor-lined gash that was thing's face. The creature sniffed the end of the barrel, savoring the aroma of freshly ignited gunpowder.

Then Nicki pulled the trigger.

A blast erupted from the gun that nearly removed the creature's head. It howled in agonizing pain, reeling backward from the impact. The side of its misshapen skull gaped open and Nicki could see that within its jaws lived row after vicious row of dagger-sharp teeth waiting to be called into action. Wet membranes hung perilously from its exposed skull, threatening to drop off completely. The beast retreated, knowing pain, serious pain, for the first time. Nicki backed away also, finally regaining some feeling in her numb legs. She pumped the gun hard again as she'd seen Lynch do, and the sound cracked loudly across the deserted cove. That sound, a warning of intense pain, drove the creature back into the ocean. Step by step, it staggered back into the protective deep. This time the salt water didn't just bring burning pain, it brought sheer torture.

As the mutant disappeared in a swirling cloud of blackish blood and saliva, Nicki collapsed on the sand. How long she lay there helpless on the beach was uncertain. The next thing she saw was a bright examination light shining in her eyes. Dr. Johann Politzer guided the light.

# CHAPTER TWENTY-ONE

—·—

M IKE RUSHED INTO THE deserted Municipal Building, barely noticing how empty it was. He ran past the sedentary Margaret at the telephones and headed straight for ballistics. The storage room was between the men's toilet and the coffee lounge. No one was in there, of course. No one ever was. Nobody ever got shot at Pine Level. They just got their heads bitten off.

Mike walked to the traffic desk and saw Brian Greenberg. Brian was the guy that ran all the routine checks on people's auto tag numbers when Brooks pulled them over. At the moment, he was trying to raise someone, anyone, on the radio.

"Problems?" Mike asked, trying to get his attention.

Brian looked up, putting the microphone down. "Can't raise the Sheriff. Been trying for thirty minutes now."

"Maybe he's away from the car," Mike offered.

"Well, of course he's away from the car. That's why I can't raise him."

"Got a minute?" Mike asked.

"For what?"

"Run a ballistics check for me?"

Greenberg shook his head. "I'm afraid I don't know diddly squat about bullets, kid," the dispatcher told him.

"You don't have to. Here." Mike handed Brian the shiny slug from the shattered camera. "Just call Tampa and give them a description of this. I want to find out what kind of gun they fired it from. Also, run a check with Tallahassee,

see what you can find on a guy named Stephen Drake. He worked out at the Triton lab. Maybe they can trace a driver's license or something. I think he's from New York."

"Sounds simple enough. I'll try it."

"Thanks Brian," Mike said as he headed for his darkroom.

"What's the matter?" Brian called after him. "Somebody fire this at you?"

"Somebody shot at my camera."

"They get it?"

Mike turned with a sad grin. "Yeah," he said. "In the heart."

"Son of a bitch!"

"Where the hell is everybody?"

"Some's out on the shark hunt. The Sheriff is on beach patrol."

"Okay," Mike said, opening the darkroom door. "If anybody wants me, I'm in the darkroom."

"Expecting a call?"

Mike frowned. "Not really, but you never know." He turned off the light.

The darkroom's coolness was a relief from the humid horrors he had encountered outside. The room was quiet, and the acrid stench of developing chemicals smelled good for a change. He may have gotten some nerve together from the frequent photography of dead bodies, but the smell of death was something he would never quite become accustomed to. He sat for a long moment in the darkened room, letting his thoughts gather. Things were just happening too quickly. Too many puzzles and too few answers. Since he had arrived, something had turned this little town on its ear. People were being torn apart in great numbers for a place that had never even experienced one murder before. And yes, he was sure that it was murder. No shark or barracuda had killed old Lankford or walked onto the deck of Ron Cananga's boat. No fish had tossed Sheila's body high on the jetty rocks, and no squid had taken a shot at him a few hours ago. Animals were dumb creatures, killing only for survival. They couldn't fire a gun. There was something cunning about all of this. Something treacherous and calculating. Something human, Mike figured.

With his arrival had come a series of mutilation deaths that rocked the tiny community, and with all that he had still found Nicki. Young, beautiful, defeated. A girl he could learn to get comfortable with. If he ever had the opportunity. She seemed to need him, want him.

A heart-breaking problem deep within her reached out to him and he couldn't help. Couldn't even let her know he was already aware. Not yet anyway. While she appeared on the verge of accepting the affection that Mike could give her, she also seemed distant. He wondered at her relationship with the women at the lab. How could anyone have perpetrated such an evil act against someone like Nicki? Mike pushed the questions from his head, but they kept coming back, gnawing at him. It was something best not thought of. He wanted nothing more than to hold her, make love to her. She didn't seem to want that level of attention. Maybe she felt dirty, unclean. Unworthy of love. Mike fought back his inner anxieties about the young girl with the golden-brown skin.

It all seemed trivial considering the wave of destruction and near hysteria that had swept over Pine Level. He needed to be more than a photographer. He needed their respect when they had none to give him. Mike needed to get involved, to help stop the killer in their midst. He hadn't wanted to get involved, but some asshole with a gun had pulled him in. Now it was impossible to pull himself out.

The ticking of the timer clock reminded him of the crushed canister of undeveloped film in his bag. He might help catch the thing that had brought horror and grief to Pine Level. Maybe Nicki would belong to him someday and he could help her forget. Right now all that mattered was getting that film into the chemical bath and coaxing up an image, if one still existed.

Perhaps hidden somewhere in those photos, unbeknownst to him, was a clue the shooter didn't want him to discover. Something hidden would turn up. He resigned himself to the task and got the job under way.

Nicki came around with a start. She tried to sit upright but only managed the raise off the slab a few inches. She surveyed her surroundings through foggy eyes and could see that someone strapped her to an examination table. The girl realized she could not rise to a sitting position and relaxed, resting once again on the soft, padded surface.

"Feeling better, young lady?" came a smooth, mannered voice.

Nicki looked away from the bright light that was shining in her face. "Yes," she said, squinting from the brilliance. She could barely make out the shape of Dr. Politzer standing beside the lamp. "The light," she said. "It hurts my eyes."

"Oh, I am sorry," he apologized. "Here, let me turn it off." He reached up and snapped the lamp off, plunging the room into near darkness, with only the slightest green desk lamp illuminating the area. It was dark and depressing. The sight of it giving Nicki an uneasy feeling.

"Some deputies on the beach found you near the point. You were in shock."

"Sheriff Lynch?" she stammered.

"Dead, I'm afraid, and from the amount of blood covering you, I would have thought you'd be dead as well."

"Not my blood," she whispered, looking down at the clean white medical gown she was wearing.

"Very fortunate for you."

"Please, I'm alright," Nicki said. "Let me up. I've got to call Mike."

"As a doctor, I don't think I'd advise that, young lady," Politzer said. "Your condition had me worried, I feared you might have lapsed into severe shock. It forced me to give you a muscle relaxant for your own good and if I let you up now, you'd almost certainly topple right over on your face. Now that would be the capper, wouldn't it?"

"I guess so," Nicki said, but somehow her muscles felt strong to her. She clenched and unclenched her fists, feeling the tightness of them. "How long do I have to lie here?" she asked.

"Oh, not too much longer. But please don't fight it. The rest is good for you."

"I have to get a message to Mike Reardon, at the Municipal Building."

"Young Reardon?" Politzer said. "I know him well. The photographer fellow from Miami, right?"

"Yes."

"Well, we've had a few drinks together since he first came here. You know, I've been helping the police with their medical questions since the town's old doctor moved on. What was his name?"

"I don't remember," Nicki muttered. "Crenshaw, I think."

"Yes, that's it. Dr. Amos Crenshaw."

Politzer walked over to the illuminated desktop and picked up a pad and pencil, bringing it back to Nicki's side. "Now then," he began. "What's the message that's so important? I hope it's not one of those mushy love things. There will be plenty of time for that when you're up and about again."

"No, it's the lab..."

"Lab? What, the Police lab?"

"No, Triton... Triton Project. Marine lab on the point."

"Okay, what shall I write?" Politzer asked.

"That thing... the creature... the one that killed Sheriff Lynch."

"Creature?" he said, shaking his head. "I was afraid of this. You're lapsing into deep shock."

"No, listen," she protested. "Something from the lab... kind of mutation... killing..."

"Well, I think a mild sedative is in order for you, young lady."

"No! You must call Mike... warn him!"

"I'll call him first thing, but right now you need rest and getting worked up will help nothing," the doctor said as he pulled out a syringe full of dark brownish fluid.

"It walked... like a man..."

Politzer raised her gown, plunging the needle into Nicki's exposed hip, emptying the syringe of its contents. "You rest now, miss. I'll take care of everything."

Her vision blurred into a swirling mass of confusing, conflicting images. First she saw Mike, smiling; then she saw the mutant grinning with half of its gigantic face blown away; she saw Dr. Politzer looking down at her and Sheriff Lynch's brain washing onto the sand. The visions swam before her eyes as she slipped under.

"Got to tell them... warn them..." she muttered, almost incoherently. "The creature... is Stephen... must be." And then she passed out.

Politzer replaced the pad and pen on the desk, having written nothing. He crossed to the telephone and dialed the operator.

"Hello, this is Dr. Johann Politzer... Could you connect me with the police... thank you." He waited for the call to go through. He heard the tired voice of Margaret on the other end.

"Sheriff Lynch, please," Politzer said, waiting for the reply. "No word from him yet? Do you suppose he'll check in later?" He listened to the reply. "Well, I suppose I'll call back then," he sighed, hanging up the phone. He looked over towards Nicki, who lay bound unconscious on the examination table. "They still don't know that fat fool is dead," he said with smug satisfaction.

# Chapter Twenty-Two

—·—

C APTAIN MILLER'S OLD TUG, the Maybelle, cruised the shoreline for hours. The hunters had exhausted their beer supply, and the fun had faded. Had it not been for Lynch's strict orders to continue the hunt until he radioed, it would have ended long ago.

"Where the hell is the sheriff?" one deputy grumbled.

"Fuck if I care," was the overall consensus.

No one was even searching the waves any longer. No one cared. The afternoon dragged on like a late-night movie and thoughts of returning to town for some serious drinking were on everyone's mind. The stench of the chum was overpowering, even after most of it had been dumped overboard.

Big Ed had signed aboard with his shotgun and big mouth and he made it a point to irritate somebody at every opportunity. He complained about missing work, although he hadn't held a job in over a month. He complained about leaving his green-eyed Robin alone, since he was certain every toothless mother's son in Pine Level had the hots for her, but mostly he complained about the minor stipend that was being offered by Lynch for his services. Deputy Nicholas told him to pipe down and do his job, and while Big Ed knew better than to start something, he wasn't about to pipe down.

It stumped Captain Miller. Something should have come after the bait, but the sea was motionless. Not a single living thing splashed on the surface. But Miller and the others had their orders and the old Captain didn't mind. He was being paid well to drag these sorry losers around in a relentless circle and business had been slow since people started turning into bait.

The rest of the hunters didn't see it quite the same. They were bored, sun-burnt and a little beyond drunk. These men would have blasted a pelican out of the water just for the hell of it. Miller knew they would get rowdy soon if Lynch's order didn't come, but what did he care? In a few more hours, the sun would start setting and order or not, he'd be heading back to the marina.

Since the incident on the Jenny Lynn, very few skippers were staying onboard after nightfall. Miller may have packed on the years, but he figured there were still a few good ones left and he meant to keep them.

Deputy Marty Nicholas emerged from below deck, shaking his head in disbelief. "I don't understand it, Miller," he said. "Sheriff ain't checked in for hours and I can't see the sense of touring the coast any longer."

"You reckon something's happened to Bob?" Miller asked.

"How could it? He was just patrolling the beaches for swimmers. It's kind of hard to screw that up."

"What you figuring on doing, Marty?"

The deputy looked over the water. It wasn't happening, and he knew it. "I don't know," he drawled. "I guess I'll take it on myself to call this hunting trip in for the night. This just hasn't amounted to shit."

"That's a wise move, son, since I figure us to be at least an hour out of the marina. I would love to turn her around and go home."

"I hate to override the Sheriff's orders, but I can't see any other choice. Let's do it."

"As you say, Marty." Miller nodded and ambled over to the steering cabin.

Deputy Nicholas stepped up to the stern and clapped his hands. "Men, we're packing it in. I haven't been able to contact Sheriff Lynch, but the afternoon's shot and it's a long ride home, so we're calling it a day."

The hunters voiced their support of Nicholas's decision with a round of half-hearted cheers. Even Big Ed seemed happy, but their shouts of approval quickly turned into shrieks of panic when the boat heaved suddenly to one side.

Water rushed over the decks, taking many of the men off their feet. Within seconds, the boat had righted itself while the excited cries of the frightened men filled the air. Those still standing rushed to help those who fell. Nicholas himself had gone overboard and was floundering in the gulf somewhere off the bow. The craft sat motionless for only a few seconds before lunging to the opposite side. The sound of rending wood and metal added to the chaos as it threw the men off their feet.Captain Miller was on the wheel in the steering cabin. He hooked his arm through it, struggling to remain upright during the severe jarring of the vessel. Something tremendous was ramming the bottom of the boat. A whale perhaps, but impossible under the circumstances. If such a thing had approached the craft, someone would have sighted it.

A whale in these waters would be news any day, but right now it was inconceivable. A variety of panicked thoughts rushed through Miller's brain as he clung to the wheel of the lurching craft. One was he was about to die.

The boat righted itself and the shaken men scrambled to throw a life preserver over the side to their comrade. Marty Nicholas saw the preserver splash about ten feet from him and swam for it. A rope trailed from it to the boat and one mate stood ready to pull him in as soon as he could secure a grasp on the floater.

It took only a few strokes to reach the hoop-like supporter, and Nicholas soon had it over his head and placed beneath his arms.

He signaled the man to reel him in with a wave of his hand, then vanished beneath the surface. The mate stood staring at the churning waters that had replaced the deputy's position and felt a powerful pull on the line. It was as if a large fish had taken the deputy-bait on the line and was fighting with the angler. The rope jerked from the mate's hand with a ferocity that brought fresh blood rushing from his fingers. The line twisted and dove deep before resurfacing and circling again. By this time, others gathered at the side to observe the wild display while they helped the remaining men back on board the weakened craft. After a few moments, the rope became still, then Deputy Nicholas burst through the surface, screaming.

Most of his face was gone, as were his arms and legs. Something stripped away the skin around his mouth, revealing a bloodied, grinning set of raw teeth exposed to the roots. He could no longer form words, but an ugly bone-chilling cry rose from his throat before something dragged the sickening vision beneath the surface for good.

Miller heard a cry below deck and looked away from the horrifying scene.

"We're taking on water, Captain!" the man shouted.

The old man pushed past the white faces, who clung to the rail for support and jumped down below as quickly as his aching legs would carry him. What he saw there made his eyes grow wide. Water. Lots of it. Pouring in through an ugly crack in the hull. The old Captain knew the hull had been recently strengthened, but it was no match for the force they were up against. If something didn't happen soon, the boat was going down. That thought brought more terror to the Captain than he had ever experienced before.

"Get that goddamn pump going," he yelled.

"I'm trying," the mate replied. "But I don't think it's got enough power!"

"It damn well better! Otherwise, we'll all be swimming out there with the deputy."

"Maybe we can get out enough to keep us afloat until we reach the marina," the man shouted.

"To hell with the marina!" Miller shouted in desperation. "We're heading for shore. We'll ground her!"

The mate gave the pump engine cord a hard yank, and then another before he got it started. The pump, rusty from years of use, sounded like an old lawn mower.

"Keep that sonofabitch running," Miller screamed above the racket. "I'm going topside to organize everybody. Stay with that pump."

"Aye, Captain."

Then the hull caved in.

The sea water gushed through a new gaping hole, this one created by a large black leathery arm that protruded from it, clawing at anything within reach. It grabbed the mate by the forearm and dragged him into the hole. Blood mixed with sea water as the hull filled.

Miller backed toward the hatch, staring at the impending disaster. He lunged for a speargun that was strapped beside the ladder and waded through the knee-deep crimson water towards the helpless man. With a horrendous crunching, twisting sound, the mate's arm was ripped from its socket and sucked outside with tremendous force. The Captain stepped over the screaming man, shoving the speargun into the jagged wound in the hull. His finger pulled at the trigger, sending the spear bursting through the hole. The shaft traveled only a short distance before lodging in its target. The butt-end of the spear remained inside the hull.

Whatever Miller hit backed away, and the spear disappeared. The water kept pouring in, but the attacker seemed to be gone. Miller threw a worried look at the dying man thrashing about in the rising water at his feet, then hurtled topside.

"Get a move on, men, if you want to save your skins," he shouted. "We're sinking fast!"

This news panicked everyone, since they knew what going into the water meant. The more stalwart men stepped forward to help. One of them was John, a boy who could not have been over nineteen.

"What can I do?"

"Grab a few of these weak-kneed sissies and pull off that aluminum sheet," he said, showing the boat's rate sign. "Get it down below and try to patch that hole. It's our only chance."

"Yes, sir," John snapped, leaping into action.

"Nails are in the lower toolbox, but hurry. We're taking on water fast and the pump is on overload. That sign won't stop it, but we might still make it back in one piece."

John and another man ran down into the flooding hull, eager for the task. Miller looked over the rest of the ashen faced passengers.

"The rest of you," he directed. "Start throwing everything overboard that ain't nailed down. Something's trying to sink us and I'll be damned if I'm going down without a fight."

The hope of surviving spurred the men into action and within moments they were hurling the Captain's belongings into the sea.

"Who knows first aid?" Miller shouted. One of Lynch's remaining deputies raised his hand. "Good. Get below and see if you can help my mate. He's lost more than blood, but maybe you can do something for him." The deputy jumped down into the hold, but the Captain knew his man was as good as dead.

Down below, John and the other man were trying to restrain the incoming flow, fighting against the already waist-deep water that filled the bottom-most portion of the craft. Beside them bobbed the mate, face down like a flotsam. The deputy came down the ladder and sized up the situation. He waded into the hold and grabbed the dead man by the collar.

"No use bothering with him," John said. "He's done. Give us a hand here."

The deputy waded over to them through the floating debris filling the hull. "Lean into it and I think we can get it," John said. All three men pushed on the metal sign as they pounded in the nails. Within moments, the sign was in place. It bulged inwardly, perilously, but looked like it might hold.

"That might do it," the deputy said hopefully. "Maybe."

Miller came down the ladder to check the progress. "We've lightened her up on top. You boys got things squared away down here?" he asked.

"I think so, Captain," the youth answered. "But I wouldn't give it much chance of withstanding another jolt like the one that put it there."

"You're right, son, but I think it's finished... whatever it was."

The four men locked eyes on the bulging metal plate that held back the sea. Water still seeped in around the edges, but it held for the moment. There was enough daylight to steer by and, with luck and a lot of prayer, they might make it.

Miller climbed the ladder to the upper deck, hobbling past the cold, frightened faces that looked up at him for strength and reassurance, but he was empty. He had nothing left to give them. They might hold on to their lives, and that was enough.

The shadow moved along the sandy ocean floor. They hurt it. In fact, it had done nothing but feel pain for the last few days. Humankind, it was learning, could be every bit as savage as its instincts taught it to be. Now its head was alive with a torturous burning pain. A vicious, swirling agony that blotted out most of its thoughts. Some girl blasted away half its face and now there was a three-foot metal spear protruding from its eye.

As it swam, it could feel the sharpened prong of the spear jutting out the back of its head. It created a dizzying sensation, but it knew better than to pull it out. Something told its murky brain that such an action would only bring more agony.

It needed help. Help to remove the spear, to mend its face and patch up the gaping holes that riddled its body. It didn't know where to turn or who might be a friend, but something in the back recesses of its brain, back in those areas as yet unreached by the shotgun lead or the spear tip, there was a growing urge to return. Back to where it all began. Where it had first escaped into the world. If there was any help to be had in this unreasoning world of violence and hatred, it might be there. It knew, and it went.

# Chapter Twenty-Three

— · —

M IKE KICKED THE DARKROOM door open, tired, disappointed and angry. The film he tried so desperately to
salvage was ruined. He wanted it to be fogged around the
edges, but that wasn't the case. Whatever the gunman
had wanted to conceal by destroying Mike's camera, he
had done it with outstanding success. Perhaps the medical
report on the body would turn up something that Mike had
failed to see during his quick survey of the scene. Maybe the
evidence was still there to be had, but through a different
approach. He would have to wait until Dr. Politzer showed
up to make sense of the mounting carnage.

Mike walked into the officer's lounge to rustle up a cup
of coffee. His eyes were strained from the darkness of the
developing room and his back ached. The combination of
the bait shop shoot-out and the mess on Cananga's boat
had taken its toll. He was worn out and hungry. He looked at
the clock on the wall. Five o'clock. He hadn't heard anything
from Nicki. She had been so insistent about not being left
alone, he could hardly imagine she had not tried to contact
him. Maybe Greenberg on the desk had gotten a call and
been waylaid by other business. Mike looked in the dispatch
room where Brian sat, ear glued to the telephone. On seeing Mike, he finished up his call and swiveled in his chair
towards him.

"Any calls for me?" Mike asked.

"Not a thing. Got lots'a calls, though."

"More trouble?"

"Shit. I don't know. Everybody's looking for Sheriff Lynch, and that bunch that went shark hunting are overdue, too."

"Something's happened to the Sheriff?"

"Hell if I know, he ain't called in and nobody's seen him. Ain't heard from the Maybelle either, but I reckon that beat-up radio of hers just gave out."

"Still," Mike said. "It wouldn't be like Lynch to stay out of communication."

"Meaning what?" Brian was sitting up a bit more attentively.

"Meaning I think someone ought to go look for him."

"Ain't nobody to go. The boys went on the boat."

"I'll take a drive around and look for myself," Mike said. "Did Bob say where he was going?"

"Routine beach patrol he said. Reckon you'll have to check them all."

"If any of them come back, send them out immediately."

"Don't know if I can take any orders off you, kid," he said with grudging respect.

"That's not an order, Brian. It's just good sense. We need to locate the Sheriff. He might be hurt, or worse."

"I reckon it's as you say, son."

Mike turned to leave but remembered something he had wanted to ask the clerk. "Any word on that slug I gave you?"

"Oh, yeah. I almost forgot," he replied, sifting through the rift of messages on the desk. "Here it is." He handed the paper to Mike.

"It's a United States Government issue, Special Forces. But that's about all. They said we'd get a full report tomorrow."

Mike studied the note. "This doesn't tell us much, but I'll bet my paycheck it's going to," he grumbled.

"Maybe so, maybe not," Brian added. "But it tells me one thing for sure."

"Yeah? What's that?"

"Nobody around here has a gun like that. Not even on the squad. Shooter must be from out of town."

"Well, that's something. Anybody new to these parts?"

"Just you and some vacationers like that doctor fella, Politzer."

"Politzer...," Mike muttered to himself. "Where is he staying?"

"I believe he's out at Doc Crenshaw's place. He's been sorting through the mess there trying to organize the old medical charts for the new guy."

"Get me the directions. Maybe I'll stop by. I want him to check that dead guy, Lankford. There might be something special about that body. Something worth shooting a man over. Any info on Stephen Drake?"

Greenberg picked up another scrap of paper. "College guy from NYU. Came down here about a year and a half ago. Been quiet since then. Brooks gave him a speeding ticket about three months back. Nothing else," he said, reading it off the notes.

"Any family?" Mike asked, remembering Sylvia's explanation of Drake's absence because of an ailing mother.

"Nope. Says here both parents were killed in a vehicular accident in '73. Went through school on a trust fund."

Mike tapped the counter with his knuckles, thinking, then turned and rushed out the door.

Within minutes, Mike had Brian's hand-scrawled map in his fist and headed across the parking lot towards the waiting Corvair. Night was approaching fast, and he felt a tremor of apprehension run through him like a chill as he considered what else might have happened that day.

Nicki had vanished, and Lynch and his deputies were missing as well. He didn't enjoy thinking about the people who had sailed off that afternoon, now long overdue. That problem would have to be someone else's. Right now, he was only interested in locating the Sheriff.

Mike drove by Nicki's bungalow on the way and sank even deeper into despair at the sight of the lightless cottage. He stepped inside and found things to be as he had left them. She had not returned during the day, that he was sure of.

If she had, something would be out of place. Mike's photographic memory assured him that every item was as it had been when he was last there. Perhaps somewhere along the beach, he would find the answer to both mysteries.

He drove down the gulf road, feeling the oncoming chill of the night. He decided he would put the top up when he stopped.

Checking beach after beach, Mike saw little hope in discovering the whereabouts of the missing people. It wasn't until he spotted Lynch's car parked near the Point that his efforts seemed to pay off. The car was as it had been. Windows rolled down and everything. Mike touched the hood of the car. It had been cold for many hours. Before him stretched the inlet, a black-blue bay that became eerie in the twilight. Mike walked towards the water, almost hypnotically. He was becoming very cautious of the ocean. He knew a great danger dwelt there, somewhere, in the depths. Waiting.

Lynch's body had moved a little throughout the afternoon. The waves that shifted the corpse washed away most of the blood. Mike approached the body, knowing damn well the man was long dead. He saw that gaping cavity that had been the top of Lynch's head. Now hollowed out by the cleansing waves and helped along by the small crabs that scurried in and out of the skull, grabbing and fighting over tidbits of brains and flesh.

The blood had soaked into the sand, creating a large brownish stain on which the Sheriff lay. His shotgun was already showing signs of corrosion from the salt water.

Mike saw nothing to show that Nicki had been there. Nothing except the small scrap of cloth he picked up and inspected in the fading light. He recognized it as the Triton Project emblem and wondered what the connection might be between the lab and Sheriff Lynch's death.

Mike remembered Nicki's unbelievable story about the experiments that went on there and the mutated creatures they attempted to breed, and while he hadn't given her story much credence, he was wondering about it now. Could these women have created something in the lab that could cause wanton destruction? If so, and it had escaped, why hadn't they reported it? They must have known the danger, the horror, they might be unleashing.

Maybe they knew but didn't care. Maybe there was a coverup going on. Could Nicki be involved in this horror? She appeared nervous in the presence of Gail and Sylvia, and for good reason. She had been involved in the lab's work and her knowledge must've been such that Sylvia thought to blackmail Nicki with those degrading photographs. Mike wondered if he wouldn't find Nicki at the Triton Project lab now. It would bear checking out, but for the moment he needed to do something about the Sheriff.

He dragged the dead man's body up the beach, away from the surf. By the time he had reached the car, the sun had dropped, and it had thrown the beach into total blackness. Mike radioed the station from Lynch's car and heard the harrowing story of the assault on Captain Miller's boat. The deputies had made it back, but Nicholas hadn't been so lucky, he was told.

He explained the situation to Greenberg and a couple of cars dispatched. When they arrived, Mike brought the pale-faced deputies up to date on what he knew about the Sheriff's death and hurried on to notify Dr. Politzer of the rising body count.

The night had the coldness of death about it. Even with the top up, the vintage Corvair allowed icy blasts of air to whistle through the car, prickling the already rigid hairs on the back of Mike's neck. Ever since the afternoon's gunplay, Mike had been carrying his service revolver. For the first time, it felt good snuggled under his arm. He had never been keen on carrying; shooting photographs being his most cherished way of expressing himself, but now, in the wake of all the mayhem, it didn't seem like such a bad idea. He didn't want to hurt anybody, but he didn't want to die.

He had decided the pacifism bullshit his yuppie buddies had force-fed him in school just didn't amount to beans out here in the wilderness. Here, you had to be ready for anything.

By the time the Corvair pulled up to Doctor Crenshaw's place, Mike was itching for a fight. His nerves were taunt but reassured by the bulge under his jacket. He would give Dr. Politzer the message, make sure he was bundled off towards the station, then head to Lighthouse Point and the Triton Project Lab.

The lights were dim inside as Mike approached the concrete and cinder block porch that fronted the house. It was much larger than he had imagined it would be. An obvious holdover from Pine Level's earlier days when the area's economy had been more promising. He rang the bell when he didn't see the doctor's car.

No one answered.

Mike rang it again and a third time. There was a parting of the curtains in the living room window and considering the dire circumstances, he didn't feel awkward about taking a peek inside. Maybe Politzer had dosed off in front of the TV and didn't hear the bell. He looked into the darkened room and saw it was empty.

There were no furnishings, rugs or anything. Strangely enough, it appeared as if Politzer had removed everything belonging to the previous tenant, an astounding feat considering the wreckage that had consumed the place.

Something had once been in the room, Mike surmised. He could discern the outline of a rectangular carpet and where a bookcase had once sat on the discolored flooring. Of particular note was the one solitary item that lay in the otherwise barren space. It was dark, but the shape looked familiar. Mike strained his eyes to make out the silhouette. It was rounded, with tubes and gleaming chrome fixtures. A glow coming from down a hallway cast a faint halo of light around the object and he could recognize it as a scuba diving tank... Nicki's.

Even in the darkness, he was certain of its origin. He wasn't sure why it was there, but Nicki was missing and Mike was determined to follow any clues offered to him.

Mike tried to find an open door or window on the exterior of the old block home. He could break in if need be. This was not Dr. Politzer's house. It belonged to the errant Doctor Crenshaw. Politzer was there by the good graces of Sheriff Lynch, and now that he was dead, his authority was drastically diminished.

If Mike was correct, the same might be true of the missing Dr. Crenshaw as well. He looked around, laying eyes upon a discarded shovel, rusty with age, sunk deep into some forgotten flowerbed. It looked about right for the job, Mike thought, and gave it a mighty swing, sending it flying through the kitchen window. He reached inside through the jagged glass fragments and unlatched the door.

The kitchen, he observed, was barren as well. A quick check of the cabinets bore out his guess. The cupboards, like the living room, seemed to have been cleaned out. It was a strange feeling that crept over Mike as he stood in the deserted house. Only the glare of a bare overhead bulb illuminated the scene, lending an unsettling quality to the room.

He moved towards the doorway that led to the rest of the house. By the refrigerator he paused, hearing the gentle purr of the device. Odd that it should still be on in a place devoid of comfort or convenience. Perhaps Politzer kept his food in here; he was roughing it with his wife away, he had said. Maybe he was a bachelor at heart and loath to do any real cooking. Crenshaw's family, if he had one, might have removed everything from the house if they, like Mike, had guessed he would never show up again to reclaim them.

Mike opened the refrigerator door and looked inside. To his surprise, it, too, was empty. The interior was lit by a small bulb and showed every square inch of its sparkling clean emptiness. All the racks were in place, dazzling. It was as if someone had polished the metal, but of course, that was absurd. The icebox had to be at least seven years old, yet there it was. Clean as a whistle. Upon closer observation, Mike realized the refrigerator was not exactly empty. There on the bottom rack, just above the glass covered vegetable tray, were several small circular containers. Petri dishes, he thought they were called. The kind used in laboratory work for cultures and molds. Mike knelt down to get a closer look at the trays in the near sterile refrigerator. Something was in the dishes, but the round glass covers obscured and blurred their contents.

Whatever lived in the circular dishes was dark, blackish even. Mike could see that much. He reached out his hand and lifted the lid of one of the specimen containers. He moved with extreme caution in order not to disturb whatever was going on inside the dish. What he saw unnerved him.

Inside the glass container was a mass of stringy, slime encrusted goo that had been lifted from the crime lab at the station. It appeared to be a piece of the black, fleshy substance found wherever the latest killing had taken place. It was the same black tar-like stuff Mike had first seen hanging from the jagged boards around the hole in Lankford's bait shop. He could see that it rested in a small pool of fresh blood that coated the dish's bottom.

But it wasn't the fact that Dr. Politzer had absconded with the slimy evidence asking no one, or even that he seemed to carry out his own private experiments that troubled him. What bothered Mike was the sample of gooey flesh that sat in the pool of blood was still alive.

His eyes widened as he watched the flesh move around the dish like a snail, sucking up the blood that Politzer had placed there. It also might respond to the lid of the dish being removed. It expanded and contracted like an enormous leech, gorging itself on blood. Mike couldn't come up with a logical explanation for why the doctor would nurture this stuff and he wasn't sure he approved either, but that wasn't for him to decide. Gently, he replaced the lid on the dish, wondering whose blood might be at the bottom of those containers.

After a moment of contemplation, he remembered his reason for breaking into the house. He walked into the deserted living room and knelt beside the scuba gear. Dragging it into a better light, he could see clearly that it did, in fact, belong to Nicki. Her initials were clearly embroidered on one strap, just below a large bloodstain. There was oxygen in the tank, so Mike guessed Politzer had not found it in the ocean. His fear of Nicki being another casualty was not entirely put to rest, but he didn't believe she had fallen prey while diving. Surely an attack would have caused the tank to disgorge itself if the owner had been violently jerked away while in use. There were no obvious marks or scratches on its surface. Mike left the gear where it was and searched the rest of the house.

On the first level, he found little to explain why Nicki's tank would be there. The other rooms were like the first, empty as if they had dragged a giant vacuum across the place. Upstairs, Mike could see a glow emanating from the right of the stairs. He drew his revolver and climbed the steps.

Stairs frightened him as a child and were unusual in Florida. His most vivid memories of stairs were as a child in Ohio. As a boy, Mike always imagined he saw someone moving across the stairs, just out of the corner of his eye. Stairs had always terrified him and he flashed on this as he neared the top. Thinking ahead, he cocked the hammer back on the .38. The noise seemed almost deafening in the quiet of the empty house. The sound echoed off the walls of the uncarpeted rooms. To his relief, nothing jumped out at him when he reached the top step.

He crept to the open doorway that glowed like a dim beacon. He thought, here was a room with something in it. As he approached the door, he could see they set it up like an operating theater. Equipment and chrome tables lined the walls, giving the quarters an alien appearance. The metal reflected in his eyes, which had already become accustomed to the dimness of the house.

It took him a few seconds to look past the glittering machinery and polished metal that sparkled in his eyes, but when he could see, a familiar shape became apparent. It was strapped to a padded table. Taking a few steps forward, he could see it was human. A few steps more and he realized it was Nicki.

He rushed to her.

"Honey, wake up. It's me," he urged, pulling at the buckles that held her tight. She stirred a little.

"Where am I?" she moaned, shaking her head, trying to regain her senses.

"They told me this was Dr. Crenshaw's place, but I guess Politzer's been camping here," Mike said, loosening the belts as fast as he could.

"Dr. Politzer..." Nicki muttered.

"Yeah, have you seen him? Did he do this to you?"

"Yes, he brought me here... from the beach... Sheriff Lyn ch..."

"I found Lynch a few hours ago... can you sit up?"

"I think so... dizzy, so dizzy..."

"He must have given you a shot."

"Some kind of injection," she remembered.

"Why didn't he call the station... Alert someone?"

Nicki held her head in one hand, steadying herself on the edge of the table. "He told me he would call you... that's all I remember."

"Well, he's got a lot of explaining to do when I catch up with him. You should see what's going on in the icebox."

"What...?"

"Yeah, it's... " Mike's words trailed off as his eyes fell upon the ugly bruises on Nicki's arms. They were inflamed with speckled bits of dried blood still clinging to them. It didn't take a genius to realize that Politzer had been drawing blood from the drugged girl. Blood used to feed the living flesh in the petri dishes. The thought of it made Mike's temper flair. He wanted to throttle the doctor for even thinking of such a hideous act. He wondered if it had been Politzer's intention to keep Nicki a prisoner as a constant blood supply for his little pets downstairs. The idea sickened him, but at that moment, nothing seemed too farfetched. When he found Politzer, he'd get some answers.

"Can you walk?" he asked, helping Nicki to her feet.

"If it would get me out of here, I could dance," she said.

"Maybe later. Right now, let's just waltz down to the car and get the hell out of here. There are strange things going on here and I can't figure it out yet, but the farther you are away from here, the better off you'll be."

Nicki shivered as Mike ushered her outside into the night air. She wore nothing more than her bikini and Mike's jacket, which he had draped around her shoulders.

"It's going to be a cold ride to your place, but I'll try the heater and see if it works." he said half-assuredly.

Even frozen and still groggy from Politzer's drugs, Nicki protested. "I can't go home. There isn't time."

"Time for what?" he asked.

"The killer... I'm sure it's Stephen."

"Stephen Drake?"

"I found a scrap of cloth today... in the ocean... it had the Triton seal on it."

"I know, but what's the connection?"

"It was gray cloth from a surgical shirt. The kind Stephen used to wear all the time. The girls never wore them. Ever. I found it on the ocean floor. I know the shirt was his. He killed Sheila."

"So Stephen is swimming around under the ocean," Mike asked, "coming up occasionally to kill people?"

"It was the lab animal, the experiment, that got loose and attacked him. It must have infected him with the altered enzyme. Drove him crazy."

"And now he's a mutant too," Mike concluded. Now he almost believed it himself.

"I'll tell you this much," she said. "If we go to Triton, we'll find the answers, but we must do it now."

"Why now? Can't we get some back-up? I mean, I don't even have a radio in my car to call up the boys."

"I don't blame you for being afraid. I'm not a brave person myself, but I overheard the doctor on the phone with someone as I was going under. He said they were going to capture it tonight and transport it to another lab."

"Who are they?"

"I don't know, the government maybe. Politzer's working with someone. We can't let it happen. Stephen deserves better than to be caged up as an experiment."

"I'm not sure what Stephen deserves, or if he's even still alive."

"If we can get in there and prove he exists, we can blow the lid off this thing. Expose it for what it's become."

"What makes you think this monster is going to come back to the lab?"

"A phone call... the last thing I heard was the creature had broken through the metal door and was inside the building. They were going to secure that area and capture him tonight."

Mike's Corvair did a screeching U-turn in the middle of the deserted shoreline road. Triton it would be, he decided. What other choice did he have? If Nicki was right, they'd have to work fast. He had no delusions of capturing or killing the beast, but if they could catch Politzer and his buddies in the act, then they'd have to come clean and maybe the affair would finish with a little outside help.

The gun under his armpit felt like a leaky ice pack. He hoped that feeling would go away soon, and it did. Pure, undiluted fear replaced it.

# CHAPTER TWENTY-FOUR

— · —

T HE PAIN IN SYLVIA'S arm throbbed as consciousness crept back into her brain. She had been out for some time, but the racket coming through the intercom would wake the most sedated body. It was a loud, irritating sound. Not unlike that made by a tremendous automobile accident. The crash of breaking glass and rending metal echoed through the tinny-sounding speaker, but it was impressive. As she opened her eyes, a maze of swirling, out-of-focus images swam in front of them. She was expecting to see Gail, but this was not the case. Someone else was in front of her, looking into her dilated eyes. Someone unfamiliar to her. She blinked a few times, trying to conjure up a clearer view of the room. Objects came out of the fog and took on more definite, identifiable shapes. Someone grasped her wrist and clenched it.

Dr. Politzer pressed his fingers into the soft skin about her wrist and timed her pulse. "You're doing much better now," he said.

"Who are you?" Sylvia mumbled.

"I'm Dr. Politzer, my dear. How are you feeling?"

"Alright, I guess. Sleepy."

"And wellyou should be. Miss Anders informed me of the heavy sedative she had administered to you. By my count, you should still be out."

"I want to sleep... please," she said, barely hanging on.

"Well, I'd like to oblige, but I'm afraid that's impossible. If you value your life, you must do as I say. Your experiments seem to have gotten out of hand and need immediate attention."

"Experiments...?"

"Yes, you remember, don't you?"

"Of course..." Sylvia stammered, trying to force clear thoughts back into her skull.

"Good," Politzer smiled. "That's a start. Now let me put it into perspective for you. Your lab assistant, Stephen, I believe Gail said his name was... the mutant specimen infected him. He's back inside the building and very upset. Now I don't blame him, but he would like to tear your head from your body... given an opportunity, of course. My concern is only for your welfare and that of your associate, Miss Anders."

"Gail..." she gasped. "Where is she?"

"She's attempting to secure A Sector. That's the one nearest the bay, if I'm not mistaken. That's where your friend is. You can hear him on the intercom," Politzer said, referring to the violent smashing sounds coming through the speaker. "He's trying to break through even as we speak. The doors are holding him back, but I'm not sure for how long."

"What are you trying to do?"

"Capture him, I suppose. Get him out of everyone's hair and off to some nice safe place where he can't hurt anybody."

Sylvia pushed herself up onto one elbow, listening to the sounds of unrestrained destruction coming over the intercom. She thought clearly now and wondered about the doctor who sat in the face of approaching disaster.

"You don't look worried enough," she said.

"Oh, but I am," Politzer said. "I'm very worried. Your friend caused quite an uproar, and while it's hardly as noticeable as if it had happened in a larger community, it's gotten to a point where it will be difficult to explain."

"Just who are you?" she asked, sitting upright. Her head was spinning from the pain in her arm and the side of her face, but she sensed a lot was at stake here.

"I'm Dr. Politzer. The Foundation is where I work. I came into town as soon as rumors got back about your minor mishap. I've waited and watched, gathering as much information as I could about the beast. Its patterns of behavior. It surprised us you two never reported the accident to the head office. That was very inappropriate for you."

"We didn't know what to do," she explained. "And besides, all the experiments had died after a short while. We figured it couldn't survive on its own for long."

"But you were wrong. It survived and grew... flourished even. Now that's encouraging."

Sylvia eyed the timid-looking doctor. What was he getting at? Even in her groggy state, she could tell the man was talking in circles and she didn't trust him. Something in his eyes gave him away. Something cruel and malingering. She knew this man could and would kill if necessary. Her nerves drew at her very fiber. For all his calmness, Sylvia knew he was desperate.

"What do you intend to do?" she asked.

"The government wants him back in custody. Our custody. We're all very excited about the operation and they might even reward you despite your obvious attempts to cover up the whole situation. An armored truck is on its way here. It should arrive with a small detachment of operations personnel trained to handle situations such as this."

Politzer withdrew a cigarette from his pocket and lit it, inhaling. "This has happened before, you know."

"I don't know what you're talking about."

"Well you didn't think you were the only ones working on the Triton Project, did you? There are labs around the world working on this. We've never seen fit to put them in touch with each other, of course. It might ruin the natural progression of development, you know. In most cases, the work leads to some clandestine sort of experimentation, behind our backs and in most cases, something very similar has occurred. In fact, we were counting on it."

Sylvia looked at him. "It almost sounds as if you were experimenting on us."

"Well, that's close. We set up the operation and left you in charge of a very simple humanitarian project. You, however, took steps to further the work here beyond its logical, legal, purpose and created an indestructible monstrosity." He paused for a moment, drawing on his cigarette. "You know, I really should stop smoking - at the rate science is going, I don't think lung cancer is going to be cured any time soon."

If you don't like what's happened, destroy it."

"That's not to say such a creation is of no value," the doctor hastened to add. "In fact, we plan to transport it to a new site in the Caribbean where it will join several other experiments like it, developed under similar circumstances at our sister labs."

"What...?" Sylvia stammered.

"You should see the one the Japanese came up with. Now there's technology. Human nature led us to believe that given an opportunity, and a little rope, all the project sites would stop working on the real problem we gave them and start creating monsters. It was just too tempting, don't you agree?"

"I guess so."

"Well, either way, it solves the world's overpopulation. Crazy as it sounds. I mean, considering the fact that your project was to develop unlimited foodstuffs to feed the growing masses. In its own twisted logic - if you can't feed the hungry... you might as well dispose of them."

"That's not what we were trying to do!"

"Well, I'm making a joke, of course," Politzer said. "A bad one, but a joke just the same."

A loud crash came over the intercom. Much louder and fiercer than any preceding it. The doctor looked up at the speaker box on the wall, only slightly surprised.

"So much for the door," he said.

"Now what?" Sylvia was listening to the sounds of the creature trailing off when she asked.

"I suppose 'run for it' is too simple a phrase?"

"Let me gather some papers," she said. "I'll be right behind you."

Politzer rose to his feet, assisting Sylvia only slightly as she struggled to regain her balance. "See that you step on it," he said. "I don't think I'll be much for waiting."

Near A Sector, things had heated. Gail was clambering backwards as fast as she could over a barricade of twisted metal, her right leg bleeding profusely from a freshly opened gash. The beast lingered on the other side of the door, but the terrific force applied to tear through the jagged hole caused Gail to stumble, ripping her thigh open on a sharp piece of steel. She nursed her blood-soaked limb as best she could and crawled crab-like over the blockade. She had piled up metal chairs, empty filing cabinets, anything she could lay her hands on to reinforce the heavy door that separated the inhabited portion of the lab from their horrendous stepchild. Little by little, it pressed the door inward. Massive fists beating against the other side had weakened the strength of the thick iron and steel. Again and again it pounded. Harder, faster, and each time with more force. It knew she was there. It smelled her blood on the other side. Waiting and afraid, she knew it wanted her.

Gail had held her ground, shotgun at the ready. She had let Dr. Politzer in and almost half-believed his fantastic story. If he were telling it straight, then military support troops couldn't be far behind. Politzer said this sort of thing had happened before, but Gail wasn't sure he was being truthful. If he was, the men coming would know how to handle the situation. How long she could hold her position with the furious creature raging against the door, thirsting for her blood, she couldn't tell. She tried to keep her finger off the trigger of the shotgun for fear of accidentally discharging it, but time after time, it kept creeping back. Gail was terrified and ready to blast the first thing through that portal. In her mind, she was certain an immediate evacuation of the building was in order, but the doctor had diagnosed Sylvia as too injured to be moved. A potential blood clot might dislodge itself, travel through her blood-stream to her heart and kill her, he had said. No, they would have to hold the fort until the proper aide arrived and she could be transferred to an emergency medical unit. Now Gail wondered if she too had become injured beyond the point of escape. The blood kept coursing out through the deep wound in her thigh.

When the creature's clawed fist had first shot through the tear in the thick metal, Gail unleashed a panicked scream. The opening was not large enough for the thing to get in, but its arm waved, clutching, grasping at anything within reach. After her first flush of panic subsided, she froze, eyes locked on the two-foot-wide rip in the door. She waited, and soon the arm retreated. There was a moment of quiet and she saw the black, shiny wetness that was its face, noiselessly peeking at her through the opening. Her finger squeezed the trigger, sending a double round of buckshot through the hole into the creature's head.

The blast sent her reeling backwards off her feet. She keeled over a portion of her barricade and landed hard on her hip. The force had caused her to drag her leg across a jagged portion of one of the filing racks and a long gash, at least an inch deep and six inches long, opened up. Gail lay on her side, clutching the gaping wound on her thigh, her lifeblood racing unchecked through her fingers.

All was quiet on the other side of the door. Gail decided to return to the main lab where Sylvia and Dr. Politzer were holed up. There, at least she could get some first aid supplies to halt the bleeding before it got out of con-trol. As she dragged herself to her feet, there came an-other tremendous crash against the security door. What-ever waited beyond that barrier was not only alive but pissed-off. Shooting it in the face had made it mad, and now it was more determined than ever to get its tormentor. Gail made a strategic withdrawal with all due haste. As she hurried down the darkened corridor towards the relative safety of the lab, she could hear the door behind her give way to the relentless force beyond.

# CHAPTER TWENTY-FIVE

— • —

G RAVEL AND SHELL SCATTERED as Mike's Corvair slid into the parking lot of the Triton Project Lab. From the outside, everything seemed quiet. Not even the faintest sound issued from within. A quick survey of the cars in the lot proved one thing, however... Dr. Politzer was here.

Several irrational, mean-spirited thoughts went racing through Mike's mind as he climbed out of the car. Politzer and his apparent abduction of Nicki were at the forefront, but he pushed those into their proper perspective considering the rampaging mutant that might wait within the structure. If Nicki's suspicions were correct, it would take more than Mike's regulation revolver to bring this nightmare to an end. If what Nicki thought was true and this killer was what she said it was, it might require an entire army to bring it down. Mike wanted to get inside the complex and make that important phone call.

He helped Nicki out of the passenger seat but wasn't sure what to do with her. She seemed weakened by the blood Politzer had drained from her and the drug effects were still lingering, but she knew the combination to the lock and was knowledgeable of the layout. Besides, he thought, what if the creature wasn't inside the structure, but still on the outside? Nicki would be in even greater danger perhaps, but she would have an avenue of escape that might not be inside the sealed fortress.

Nicki had said earlier that she was not a brave person, but Mike realized the courage it took to walk into Triton.

Beyond the danger of encountering the creature, she also had to face Sylvia and Gail. The damning photos of her were only the grimy residue of the humiliation and degradation they had subjected her to against her will. If she could face that, she could face anything. Mike decided then that he would never mention the photos. He wanted to forget and help her forget. He knew in that instant she was the most important thing in the world to him. If he could, he would erase what he had seen from his mind forever.

"You've got to let me go with you," Nicki said, almost seeming to read his thoughts. "I know what you're thinking, but it's no good. You'll never manage in there without me."

"If that thing's in there, it might make your girlfriends more cooperative, you know. In fact, I'm sure they'd be glad for us to help them out right about now."

"If they've got any sense, they might not be in there, Mike," she added. "If they are, they might not be alive. You've got to let me go with you."

Mike knew he wouldn't be able to start an argument that would win over Nicki. Without another word, they walked toward the sealed doors. Nicki punched in the proper digits, and the lock responded with a series of low hums. After a few moments, the signal light flashed green, and the door swung open. Mike had expected to hear somebody's voice over the intercom, but only the rush of air pushed by.

The silence caused an annoying feeling to creep through his bones. He'd felt it before... it was terror. With no outward show of emotion, he stepped inside, gun at the ready. He motioned Nicki inside after checking the room and closed the door as she entered.

"Which way to a phone?" he asked.

She pointed to an unlocked side door.

Mike stepped through the unlocked portal into a small room similar to a radio broadcasting booth. There was one chair, a table and a telephone. It was no great surprise to discover that the line was dead.

"I guess somebody forgot to pay their bill," Mike said as he emerged from the room. She shouldn't see his true feelings at a moment like this. Mike wondered about her own cool exterior. There was a distinct lack of fear about the girl that unnerved him. He didn't like that or trust it.

"Can you use a radio?" she asked.

"Lead on."

Nicki ushered Mike down another unprotected hallway that led to a small lunchroom-type cubicle. There, among the tables and chairs, was a shortwave radio set. Mike hurried over to the device and flipped the power switch, but try as he might, he could raise no one on the receiver. He sped through all the frequencies, but it was no use. Communication in the building appeared to be blocked.

"Somebody's cutting this place off," he surmised. "They don't want a message to get out of here. Whoever is behind this has enough power to cause a radio blackout. Smells like the old government cover-up to me."

Nicki side-stepped at Mike's comment, pulling at his sleeve instead. "Let's find the others," she said. "They may be in danger."

"I think it's foolish to rush around in here without some kind of support. If we meet your monster buddy in there, I'm afraid this pop-gun of mine ain't gonna cut it."

"What's the alternative? If we leave, Gail and Sylvia might be killed and it will get away."

"If he's here at all." Mike replied, thinking for a long moment. "I guess we don't have a lot of choices, but mind you, if we find those iceberg bitches in one piece, we're hightailing it out of here. Fuck the monster, fuck Politzer, fuck everybody."

Nicki sensed Mike had resigned himself to his fate and motioned him with a flip of her hand. "If your mind is made up, follow me. I think I know where they'll be." He gave Nicki an approving nod.

"Let's go."

Dr. Politzer turned with a start as Gail burst into the lab, clutching her bloodied thigh. In his grasp, he held a high-powered government issue rifle, which he aimed at her as she staggered in.

Sylvia was up and about, gathering papers and files, but her bandaged arm was slowing down her progress. The throbbing feverish pain from the vicious bite of the dog-mutant kept her on the verge of near delirium. Only a single-mindedness towards her scientific goals kept her feet moving and even that dedication was ebbing fast.

Politzer had stood guard towards the front of the lab, gun at the ready, while Sylvia tried to collect the notes and journals required to analyze the mutation phenomenon more thoroughly. When Gail stumbled into the room, sagging towards a chair for support, Politzer turned and rushed to her side.

"Is it through the security door?" he asked nervously, hardly seeming to notice the severe injury she had sustained. His concern was not for her. "Is it inside the sector?" he demanded.

Gail just shook her head, her eyes frozen on the gurgling slash in her leg. Sylvia hobbled over as best she could, kneeling beside the stricken girl. She said to let her get a bandage.

"You get back to what you were doing," Politzer snapped. "I'm a doctor. I'll take care of it." Sylvia turned and shuffled to the desk, gathering more and more papers and files in her mad dash against time. The gouge in her cheek ached, impairing her vision, but she worked on, desperate to finish.

"The creature," Gail gasped out. "It's not far behind me, but I think it's injured."

"Injured?" Politzer asked. "Not severely, I hope."

"I tried to kill it, but it didn't seem to slow it down. There's a spear stuck in one of its eyes."

"How much time do we have?" Sylvia asked.

"Ten minutes... it wasn't through the door yet, but it had a head start on it."

"Ten minutes will be sufficient," the doctor stated. "We'll finish things here and head for the front of the building. The squad should be here."

"Squad?" Gail mumbled, her attention still focused on her wound, which Politzer was wrapping in sterile gauze.

"The doctor's playing with the big boys," Sylvia said offhandedly. "Remember them?"

"Your boss, Miss Anders," Politzer added.

"There's some big plan," Sylvia continued. "To capture that thing and ship it out of here for further study, maybe even a little cloning, eh, doctor?"

"Oh, nothing so grand, but a few more like him wouldn't be a bad idea. The War Department would jump at such an opportunity."

"I'll bet. In fact, they'd like a few more hundred of them," she replied.

"This is no time for you little 'mothers' to moralize, my dear. Now get your things together. We're moving out now."

Suddenly, the lab door caved in.

Politzer scrambled to his feet, leaving Gail sprawled across the chair as he reached for his rifle. Gail tried to rise, but her leg gave out and she crumbled to the floor, her knee twisting torturously in new and untried positions. She screamed in agony as the bandage seeped fresh blood. Sylvia jerked around to see Politzer heading for the exit, her clumsy, wrapped forearm scattering documents everywhere.

The monster burst into the room and froze. The light was much brighter here and the flurry of frightened energy being dispersed confused it. In its wounded, chopped up condition, the beast was groggy and uncertain. Objects were spinning about the room, some running. The smell of blood and infection crept into its nostrils, helping it to get a proper bearing on its surroundings. Under the bright lights, the creature's movements seemed sluggish, almost in slow motion. It was as if it were ashamed of its appearance, humbled. Darkness had provided a shroud under which to move, but now illuminated by the lab's brilliance, the beast knew others could see him as he was. More confusion poured through its bullet-riddled brain. It wanted help and had somehow thought that here within these walls help could be found, but it discovered the doors bolted. Once inside, it realized there would be no help from these humans.

Seeing that the mutation was at a momentary impasse, Sylvia rushed to assist Gail. Politzer hesitated to shoot, throwing one worried look back at both women and then towards his prized beast before making good his escape. Gail writhed on the floor, barely conscious of the thing's presence in the room. Sylvia hooked her arm under Gail's shoulder and tried to hoist the injured girl to her feet, but it was no use. Gail's mind slipped into that region known as shock and was refusing to function. Sylvia's injuries were screaming with a life of their own as she tried unsuccessfully to pull the girl to safety.

The creature looked down at them, a glimmer of recognition racing to its foggy brain tissue. It knew these people, recognized them. How or why was not a question easily answered, but it was sure some familiarity existed between them. It moved forward slowly, keeping its ever-present watery eye fixed on them. Its own blackish, stringy blood clung to the remnants of its face, magnifying its terrifying vision. The jaws opened and closed, forcing oxygen through its battered gills, unconcerned with the fact that its own blood was running into its mouth. Captain Miller's spear waved about in front of its face, still implanted in its head like Ahab's harpoon.

Sylvia tried to drag the inert Gail away from the creature but it was too much to attempt in her weakened condition. As the thing approached within three feet of the cowering forms, Sylvia gave up and released her hold on the semi-conscious girl. She scrambled backward towards the desk, grabbing a last few quick handfuls of paper before fleeing the room in the direction Politzer had fled.

The creature looked at Gail, curled up in a fetal position on the floor. It reached down and prodded her with an outstretched claw. She did not respond. Thoughts formed in the brain. Ideas swirled within the blackness. It felt compelled to spare the life whose shallow breathing was the only sound in the room beyond its own desperate gasps for air.

Something in the torn, ravaged mind said to move onward.

# CHAPTER TWENTY-SIX

—·—

N ICKI SEEMED UNABLE TO lead Mike in the right direction. For several minutes, they had searched
through the darkened building for Sylvia and Gail with
no success. Corridor passed unto corridor with no sign
of the women or Dr. Politzer. Mike thanked God that they
hadn't seen the creature either. If they were lucky, he
figured, the place would turn up empty and they could
return to the station at Pine Level and call out the Coast
Guard. Mike had never even considered the possibility
of luck, however.

The duo ran into Politzer as they took a curve in the
upper hallway. The doctor, whose scientific reserve had
been wiped away by a panic afforded only to small children, looked like he had no intention of slowing down.
Mike intercepted him by the arm. Politzer struggled for
a moment until he laid eyes on Nicki and realized he'd
been caught.

"What's the hurry, Doc?" Mike demanded, shaking
Politzer. "You got that thing on your ass?"

Politzer quivered in Mike's grasp, straining to get free.
"It's back there, but it's bigger and stronger than I expected. Nothing can stop it short of an army."

"So, what are we going to do?"

"They sent a military crew to handle it... they should be
here now... outside."

"I hate to disappoint you, but we just came that way.
You've been stood up!"

"Oh, they'll be here all right. You'll see. Now unhand me," he demanded, pressing the barrel of his rifle against Mike's ribs. "I've got to get out! They'll be waiting for me."

"Where are Sylvia and Gail?" Nicki asked.

"That way," he pointed. "But don't expect to find much of them. When that thing finishes, it's going to be headed this way."

Nicki looked up at Mike. "They might still be alive."

"Politzer," Mike said, giving the doctor a shove. "You've got some explaining to do, but I'll take it up with you outside. Get going."

The doctor backed away from Mike and Nicki, his gun still leveled at them. He turned, hurrying on towards the front of the building. The man disappeared around the corner. In his gut, he knew the doctor had been the hidden gunman from earlier in the day. His presence here at the lab also proved that he was more than just a chance visitor to Pine Level. It connected him like a grotesque Siamese twin to this thing. But it didn't matter. He'd make sure that there was time to settle up with Politzer.

"Okay, we're getting warm," Mike said. "Let's go have a look-see."

Sylvia rushed through the twisting, darkened lab corridors, caring little for the path in which her hysteria took her. As she ran, she left a scattered trail of documents about the floor... an easy map to follow for the beast that trailed somewhere behind her.

She didn't care to stop and retrieve the papers right now as each footfall increased her terror a thousand-fold. Her greatest concern right now was to escape the building alive. Making it out in one piece was more important than years of research and labor. Painful thoughts and images of Gail flashed through her mind, but she was certain her decision to abandon the girl had been the right one. Nothing more than both their deaths could have occurred by remaining any longer. How far could she have traveled if she dragged her friend away?

In the murky gloom behind her, the creature tracked its prey. It smelled the infection that was growing under the bandages of Sylvia's arm. It saw the scattered fragments of years of work on the floor in front of it, the white paper visible in the darkness. The creature stumbled on, not wanting to kill or maim, not wanting to live anymore, either. It moved forward with no idea of what would happen next.

Ahead, Sylvia stumbled onward, her heels clicking on the computer flooring. She lost track of where she was, but knew she wasn't far from freedom. As she barreled around one corner, she caught sight of Mike and Nicki coming from the opposite direction.

"Go back," she shouted. "It's right behind me!"

"What about Gail?" Nicki cried out.

"Dead!"

Mike looked down the dark stretch of hallway beyond the desperate woman, realizing his worst fears lurked there. He took a few steps past Sylvia, then turned back towards them. "You two get going," he said. "I'm going to wait here and try to hold it back."

"Mike, no!" Nicki pleaded. "We can all escape if we hurry!"

"I don't intend to stick around longer than I have to, but there are obstacles between here and the front door. No one can clear them in time if that thing's breathing down our necks. I'll be right behind you when you get out. Now go!"

Nicki fought back the urge to argue with him, but she knew he made sense. She tugged at Sylvia's elbow, setting her back into motion. "We'll wait for you by the entrance," she called back, her voice trailing off into the recesses of the complex.

Mike tensed every muscle in his body as he waited alone in the darkness for the first sight of the advancing creature. As he stared off into the shadows beyond, he wondered what it was he was up against. It occurred to him that, even though he was scared beyond words, he had never seen the enemy. He didn't know what it looked like. Whatever kind of death lurked down that corridor, he was certain, it would be wilder than his most vivid nightmare.

Politzer ran out of the complex. He stumbled for a few steps gibbering prayers like a child before being blinded by a searing barrage of high intensity quartz-lights. He threw his hands up to protect his eyes and ran forward.

In front of the Triton Project Lab was a small detachment of military personnel. The squad had set up a blockade around the front of the building, unsure of their next move. There were several jeeps equipped with heavy-duty machine-gun mounts, likewise foot soldiers knelt in various locations armed with night-scopes. Additional Infantrymen rushed from their positions towards Politzer, grasping his arms, leading him to safety.

"Who's in charge here?" the doctor demanded in between gasps.

"Colonel D. G. Jackson," answered one young private.

"Take me to him," Politzer snapped.

The soldier led the doctor to the mobile defense unit. Politzer stepped inside the vehicle. It was dark except for the ambient lights that sparkled on the control panels.

The aged and humorless Colonel Jackson was on the field telephone to home base, and nodded for Politzer to sit down, waving the private outside with a stern hand. Jackson eyed the doctor as he finished his communication, then returned the handset to its cradle.

"Who are you?" the Colonel demanded.

"Dr. Politzer... from the Foundation."

"What is the story here, doctor?" he inquired.

"It's as I reported earlier. A creature similar to the Tokyo mutation, only larger and more aggressive and, as expected, it's caused considerable damage in this area. Fortunately, this lab is so isolated the casualties have gone unnoticed by the outside media. I think there's a good chance we can settle any potential problems here, extradite the creature to the Caribbean facility and close the book on the Triton Project."

Jackson studied the doctor for a moment, puffing on a briarwood pipe overstuffed with a toasted black tobacco. He measured the coolness which Politzer seemed to impart to such trivial events as mass murder and wholesale destruction. Something dedicated to the government man beyond all good sense, Jackson figured.

He had seen Politzer's kind before. He had seen the faces of the scientists who had viewed the creature from Viet Nam. They were like children toying with a loaded gun. The excitement sparkling in their eyes, the creases that lined those same eyes from days of no sleep. It was not Colonel Jackson's place to tell the government how to conduct business, but when things got messy, he would get the call. It had been going on like this for years. Longer than even Politzer had suspected, and it would keep going on as long as somebody somewhere wanted somebody else dead.

The Colonel asked, "What are you thinking here?"

"Your goal is to capture the mutations unharmed, or at least, with as little harm as possible. A young lady wounded it with a shotgun earlier, but I think it still has plenty of fight left in it."

"Where is this young lady now?"

"Inside the building... dead, I'm afraid."

"Any other casualties? People trapped inside?"

"There were others, but I wouldn't expect to see them soon. I barely escaped."

Jackson took the pipe from his mouth and tapped the stem on the countertop. "How is it that you got yourself out and the others remained behind?"

Politzer squirmed under the piercing gaze of the officer, his mind searching for explanations. "They were the scientists who created the thing," he said, jabbering. "There were papers to retrieve, important documents. They even thought they might communicate with the creature, reason with it. I begged them to come with me, but they wouldn't listen."

"I understand," the Colonel said, but of course he didn't. He rose and walked towards the unit door. Jamming his pipe back into his clenched teeth, he stepped outside. Politzer trotted after him like a starved pup.

"A net," the doctor suggested. "A very large, heavy one made of metal chain, dropped from overhead, might do the trick. It might be possible to use its own strength against it."

"I don't think that'll be necessary, doctor," Jackson said as he walked toward the front line of soldiers surrounding the building.

"Perhaps I didn't make myself clear, Colonel. This thing is unstoppable. It doesn't seem to feel pain or injury and it is twice the size of an average man!"

"I'm pretty well versed in the series of mutations that have developed during these projects, Dr. Politzer. I believe this one is a mix of Mako shark and a male lab assistant, correct?"

"Yes, that's it," Politzer answered, surprised by the Colonel's knowledge. "So you understand the importance of being well prepared to subdue the mutant... with as little loss of life as possible, of course."

"Doctor, my orders are explicit and they don't include any capturing or subduing. This dangerous experiment has gone far enough. It might be hard for you to believe this, but nobody wants to save your baby, for study or otherwise." The Colonel turned to the Sergeant next to him. "Be standing by Hogue," he commanded. "Anything less than human shows its face in that door... well, you know what to do."

Hogue saluted. "Yes, sir, all units are ready to fire."

"Make sure you don't miss, son."

Dr. Politzer jumped forward, pulling at Jackson's shoulder. His expression was one of frustration, defeat, and anger. "You can't do this, Colonel. My orders come straight from the top. You're here to carry out the plan the way I see fit to interpret it. Do you understand?"

Jackson turned back to the aged doctor, exhaling a voluminous cloud of pipe smoke into his face. "What I understand, Doctor, is that you are under arrest. Sergeant Hogue..."

The young non-com turned. "Sir!"

"Escort Dr. Politzer here to the mobile unit and put him under guard."

"This is impossible," Politzer blurted out. "I'm one of the agency's top administrators. Not you, I'm in charge here. I can't be pushed around. Get that straight, Jackson..."

Two soldiers came up behind Politzer and removed him, cutting short the doctor's tirade. Within moments, Dr. Politzer had been whisked away.

# CHAPTER TWENTY-SEVEN

— · —

NICKI AND SYLVIA HURRIED through the last security door that stood between them and the outer lobby. Their progress had been slow along the route, hindered because Politzer had made certain every door he opened was securely re-locked. The doctor had either been afraid, or he had tried to make certain no one else could escape along the same route.

Since fleeing, there had been no sound from the receding corridors. Nicki propped each door open with a piece of furniture so Mike could escape the complex unhindered. The women ran for the front entrance after a few seconds of lock maneuvering.

They emerged into the brisk night air. The waiting soldiers helped rush them over to the emergency medical unit, where they explained the situation inside the lab to Colonel Jackson.

Nicki, especially, was relieved to hear of the arrest of Dr. Politzer. The commander listened to her story, observing the ugly needle marks the doctor had left on her arm. Her story of Politzer's private mutant lab, and Nicki's treatment, disgusted and angered the officer, who vowed to see justice done. A complete report concerning Politzer's unauthorized activities would be filed at the conclusion of the mission, he said, and proper steps taken. The officer informed Nicki that Politzer had been responsible for several unnecessary deaths in a similar incident in Toronto earlier in the year and following an investigation of that situation they

had ended all future experimental work, hence the prema-
ture termination of Sylvia's financial grant which had cost
Nicki her position. The formal withdrawal of support and
the systematic elimination of living experiments were to
include those of the Triton Project, Florida branch. Accord-
ing to Jackson, Dr. Politzer had been assigned to Pine Level
to investigate the possibilities of mutation and report back.
His report, however, showed no sign of danger and it was
only recently that he had informed Washington officials of
the new runaway breed of horror the Triton Project kitchen
had cooked up. The present order to destroy was clear
and indisputable, much to Nicki's relief. Colonel Jackson
returned to the front line as the troops waited for further
news from inside the silent complex.

Having not seen the creature emerge from the darkened
hallway, Mike edged himself back towards the front of the
building, using the doors propped open by Nicki as his trail.
It was possible, he surmised, that escape from the building
might be accomplished without ever seeing the gigantic
horror that roamed somewhere in the stillness. That was
an uplifting thought, one he cherished and nurtured. He
backtracked, keeping a sharp lookout for the unseen beast.
There was no sign of the approaching abomination after
a turn. Behind him, he could see the last door that stood
between him and escape. He suppressed an overwhelming
urge to drop his guard and run full speed for the opening.

Two steps later, the creature had him by the throat.

It had silently come out of nowhere with tremendous
speed, finding a shortcut through the building, and had got
behind Mike as he backed his way into its path. A huge,
clawed fist gripped the back of his neck, paralyzing him
from his shoulders down with its intensity. As the beast
spun him around to get a more lethal hold, Mike slipped
from its grasp. He crashed to the floor, rolling away from
the thing in one falling movement. As he tumbled onto his
back, he brought the .38 up into firing position. The target
was so large, so unearthly, Mike found it difficult to choose

any one body part of the creature to blast. He wanted to shoot holes in every living inch of the monstrosity that towered above him. Unfortunately, he only had six shots and a handful of extra shells jangling in his pocket.

The thing leaned forward, an icky drool dripping onto Mike's chest from the massive, fanged jaws above. The first resounding shot struck the creature flush in the left cheek, the blow knocking it into a spinning movement. It reciprocated by spurting blackish blood slime from the wound into Mike's face. A second shot caught the monster below the rough, sandpapery skin of its throat, opening a gaping hole through which escaping air hissed. Mike crawled back away from the confused beast, whose body seemed to be covered in gaping, bleeding, festering wounds from its previous altercations with mankind. Victory was not without its price, as the beast had always dominated its encounters with humans. Pieces of the creature's face were hanging in tatters, its gills damaged and swollen red with irritation caused by ingested pillow feathers. Large, crusted over wounds the size of silver dollars marked its chest and one eye was gone, thanks to Captain Miller's spear, which still protruded from the creature's oozing socket.

Now it looked down with its one remaining orb, watery and bloodshot beyond recognition, and tried to discern the blurry crawling shape of Mike Reardon. Somehow, it knew that the next shot to be fired into its body could be fatal. It felt weakened and ready to drop. It had to kill this human now before it dropped dead itself. The creature moved forward on slow unsteady legs, weaving as if it might topple over at any moment.

Mike seized the opportunity to rise on one knee. He shot at the thing's head. Brains and blood rained in the hallway. Mike figured a lapse in the creature's thought process might give him an opportunity to slip outside, where the odds of survival increased. As the beast reeled from two bullets in its brain, Mike made a dash for the open portal.

The creature appeared dazed as Mike approached. He had to pass by the monster to escape.

In its confused state, he thought the risk was chancy, but worthwhile. He lunged forward, gaining as much speed as he could from his kneeling position, but as he passed close to the rattled mutant, it struck out with a claw and clamped onto his shoulder, digging its talon-like nails deep into the soft muscle. Mike screamed in agony as the mutant dragged him back in front of it. With unexpected swiftness, the thing dug into his other shoulder, pulling him upward, off the floor, towards the snapping razor-lined jaws.

Still conscious, but disoriented and losing blood fast, Mike brought the gun up against the monster's chest and fired his last two rounds point blank. The creature teetered, almost collapsing, but the beast was dug down deep into its reserve for one last ounce of strength. Only a foot's distance stood between the two. Something primeval kept the behemoth going. Something would not allow it to die.

Mike's weary, blood clogged eyes strained upward into the waiting sets of rippling teeth, row upon row. What little light remained in the hallway glittered off the wet, slimy incisors, sparkling like so many tiny lights. In his clouded, unconscious mind, Mike almost fancied the sight to be attractive, and it was, until the first row of razor-sharp fangs bit into his forehead.

Blood gushed from the tender skin that stretched across his cranium as he felt it being torn loose. His next sensation was that of falling, interrupted by the hard surface of the floor slamming against the back of his skull. Blood pooled in his eyes as he squinted to look upward, his vision impaired almost to the point of blindness. He couldn't make out much, but he saw the mutation reeling on its feet, ready to drop. He watched as the monster grabbed something on the back of its head. It spun and crashed against the walls, but it was futile. Whatever was stuck could not be dislodged.

It seemed like every wound had opened again. Fresh blood and goo and gouts of thick mucus poured forth in an unending torrent of slime that sprayed out against the walls, coating everything around it in a heavy bath of sickness. The beast fell forward onto its knees, but incredibly enough, remained upright. Its head twisted back and forth, and Mike saw three lumps emerge from within the creature's skull. He watched as each lump grew larger and more pronounced. Still the monster's head twisted agonizingly, the lumps swelled, now well-defined knots of flesh, straining outward. The pressure going on inside the beast's head forced the thing's one remaining eye to extend from its socket, almost to the point of wrenching it loose.

The knots of skin stretched and squirmed back and forth as the mutant unleashed a devastating howl of pain that echoed throughout the complex. Suddenly the knots burst open, the skin splitting like rotten fruit, and Mike saw three sharpened prong-points plunge through. Metal barbs shoved outward, extending at least two inches beyond the creature's forehead, thrust through the skull... from behind.

The creature froze, feeling the force of the steel prongs through its brain, then something inside, a voice from the past, told the tortured being it was time to die. At last, peace was within its grasp. It had but to pitch forward onto its face and cease to exist.

As the beast sagged forward into a heap, Mike could see the half-crazed form of Gail crouching behind it like a madwoman. In her grip, she still clutched the handle of the large three-pronged steel spear. With an incredible surge of adrenaline, she had attempted something as hopeless as escape. Aided by the razor-forked trident, she had summoned her remaining strength, stabbing the back of the mutant's head and forcibly driving it through the layers of tough hide, bone and brain, emerging on the other side. She had killed the unkillable. The sight of the dead creature drained all of her will and she herself collapsed but a few yards beyond the fallen titan, a childish giggle escaping from her lips.

Mike wiped the congealed blood from his eyes and crawled forward, past the inert giant, to Gail's side. He had believed her dead, but somehow here she was, saving his life at the last possible moment. His shoulders ached from the deep rending gouges, but losing blood helped numb the pain. He drew his arms around the brave girl's waist and hoisted her to a semi-standing position. She was out cold, so he dragged her the remaining distance to the entrance. Hopefully, there he could get some help.

As he exited the complex with his unconscious partner, Mike was more than happy to see the combat attachment ringing the building, guns leveled in his direction. Helping hands soon lifted Gail to the medical unit and Army doctors were wrapping Mike's injured shoulders and head. Upon command, Colonel Jackson sent a clean-up crew of infantrymen into the complex with flame-throwers. No surviving experiments of any sort were to remain alive. "Incinerate everything," was the order.

They informed Mike that most of the police force of Pine Level had been lost at sea or injured during the boating expedition on Miller's boat. The Triton Project would be closed and a cover-up would protect all departments involved. They suggested that Mike and Nicki cooperate with the authorities to their own benefit. Dr. Politzer and Sylvia Trent would be dispatched back to Washington where some explanations were required. Politzer's collection of petri dish pets would be burned as well. The medics transported Gail Anders to the Veteran's Administration Hospital in St. Petersburg, where every effort was made to save her leg.

Jackson's men busied themselves sealing the dark complex, including the ocean side portals, with thick steel plates. Several soldiers reported hearing strange sounds from beyond the secured doors, but the incinerating crews inside could substantiate none of their claims. Newspapers, both local and statewide, ran minor stories on the mysterious closing of the once promising marine project, but they made little of the many lives that were lost or of the military power later employed to demolish the building through heavy explosive charges. Rumors concerning the horrors created there spread, but these stories, like folk tales, eventually found their home in cheap saloons, where they were whispered to anyone who could afford the price of a drink.

They held Mike Reardon in isolation for several weeks following the incident while debriefing took place. He was discharged and reassigned to Ft. Lauderdale, where he could realize his true ambition... that of making love to Nicki Prescott. He became the Assistant Chief Photographer - Fingerprint Division for the County of Broward and married the tanned biologist with the great breasts.

Colonel Jackson returned home to his wife and the unfinished novel he was working on, awaiting his next mission.

Sylvia Trent died after departing the Triton Project site under the care of Dr. Johann Politzer. The wound under her bandages took on a terrible life while she was being transported. Without warning, the dressing ripped open with tremendous force and a macabre new form of mutated life was born from within the infected bite that had festered there. Sylvia screamed in torturous agony as the tiny creature wiggled and strained to free itself from her flesh. Bursting forth in a shower of blood and slime, it leapt upon the horrified Dr. Politzer, biting into the soft tissue of his esophagus. The doctor's scream alerted the soldiers who tried to kill the mutant creature as it burrowed into his throat and re-emerged through Politzer's gaping mouth. Sylvia Trent died of shock and blood loss. The Mutant-spawn escaped by breaking through the vehicle window, never to be seen again.

# ABOUT AUTHOR

Fred Olen Ray is an Emmy Award winning filmmaker with over one hundred and fifty motion picture and television credits. He has directed a wide variety of films with stars such as Telly Savalas, Lee Van Cleef, Steven Seagal, Chevy Chase, George Hamilton, Cliff Robertson and Morgan Fairchild. He has written for publications as ADVENTURES IN THE TWILIGHT ZONE, WEIRD TALES, ARGOSY MAGAZINE and DISCIPLES OF CTHULHU.

His new book, WRITING THE PERFECT CHRISTMAS TV MOVIE (2021) was an Amazon #1 Best Seller for six weeks.